22
B
7

D1099426

FAIRLIGHTS

The fortified pele tower of Fairlights, its beacon shining out across the harbour, has guarded Whitcliff for centuries. Sorcha Ravell thought she'd recruited the perfect restoration expert in Nick Marten — but he turns out to be dangerously attractive; knows more about her than she can account for; and is very, very angry. As the autumn storms build and the tension rises, Sorcha must overcome a paralysing physical fear and confront a terrifying mental enigma. What happened to her so many years ago? And why can she not remember?

JAN JONES

FAIRLIGHTS

Complete and Unabridged

LINFORD
Leicester

First published in Great Britain in 2013

First Linford Edition
published 2015

A catalogue record for this book is available
from the British Library.

ISBN 978–1–4448–2404–9

Published by
F. A. Thorpe (Publishing)
Anstey, Leicestershire

Set by Words & Graphics Ltd.
Anstey, Leicestershire
Printed and bound in Great Britain by
T. J. International Ltd., Padstow, Cornwall

This book is printed on acid-free paper

1

A house on a cliff in the mist.

That's how I first saw Fairlights, at the admittedly impressionable age of four. We had driven overnight from London — Finn and I asleep in the back of the car for most of the way — and had taken a wrong turning somewhere towards the end. It meant we swooped down through the harbour village of Whitcliff and then back up again towards Fairlights instead of arriving sedately by the normal road.

I woke, sleepy-eyed, to see the crenellated pele tower rising rose-tinted out of a dawn sea-fog, and found the house entirely magical. I'm still much of the same mind now, twenty-six years later. Just walking across the wooden boards of the veranda and opening the porch door onto the plain homeliness of the stone-flagged farmhouse passageway fills me

1

with a sense of holidays and history and endless summer adventure, all wrapped up in the certainty that anything is possible.

Fairlights stands on the cliff above the village. The medieval pele tower, like all the fortified houses along the wild, broad ribbon of borderland between England and Scotland, was designed to keep its inhabitants safe from marauders. Ours (sorry, I get a little ancestral-ish when talking of the family) also had a beacon on top called the Fairlight, hence the name of the house. The Fairlight was used at night in conjunction with the Outer Light in the bay to aid navigation. This stretch of the west Cumbrian coast can be tricky. The fishermen lined the lights up by eye, one atop the other, to guide their boats past the treacherous off-shore rocks and safely into Whitcliff.

Strangely, I was never fired up by the pele itself when I was a child. Finn and our cousins — boys the lot of them, blond and good-looking like every Ravell man ever — could play at knights and castles without end, defending the tower from whoever had drawn the short straw to be the enemy force that day, but it never appealed to me. No, it was those twin lights shining out across the sea and guiding sailors home that always captured my imagination. I'd sit with a book in my hand, curled up in my window seat above the warmth of the kitchen, staring out at the dappled, wave-flecked, ever-changing sea, reading and dreaming, reading and dreaming.

The Outer Light was automated years ago, but the Fairlight is only used in emergencies these days, made redundant by widespread GPS and the bright arc of street lighting around Whitcliff harbour. Each summer, though, we'd take the rowing boat out beyond the rocks by daylight and chant the traditional rhyme whilst lining up the pele tower above the light buoy:

> *Outer to port*
> *Fairlight ahead*
> *Bring them together*
> *Home you are led*

Using those sight points alone, we made it back without a scratch every time. Fairlights has been home to many generations of Ravells. The pele tower must have looked impressive when it was first built, massive, commanding and protective on the cliff top. The problem, of course, is that four-foot-thick walls of native sandstone don't make for very large internal rooms. Our family papers report that the accommodation could become rather cramped during times of fecundity. The records, I should add, are in general a masterpiece of understatement regarding domestic matters.

The pele tower was eventually added to in the 17th century by attaching a good-sized farmhouse and outbuildings. I imagine the family breathed a collective sigh of relief. It was extended again in the 1800s by a Ravell who had a run of luck at the gaming tables before eloping that same night with an heiress. With fancy footwork and hard riding, he managed to keep hold of both fortune and bride, the pair of them arriving safely at Fairlights, wedded and bedded, one step ahead of their several pursuers. To celebrate his good fortune, he commissioned an elegantly anachronistic Regency ballroom wing, complete with supper room, card room and guest bedrooms. Scandalised local reports of the time would have us believe that the parties went on for days. The family records, disappointingly, simply mention that the new Mrs Ravell received a number of visitors on the occasion of her marriage.

Finally, in the early 20th century, a wide Edwardian veranda was wrapped around the whole building, facing the sea on two sides of the house and the gardens on the rest. The whole effect is quite beautiful.

The fact that Fairlights is flat-out impossible to run with any degree whatsoever of economy never worried me when I was young. Holidays were idyllic and endless. I always remembered that wonderful moment of arrival — the sound of the sea shurrushing against the cliff, my grandmother's sad eyes relaxing into a smile, aunts and uncles drifting onto the veranda to absorb my parents into their midst, cousins grabbing our hands and dancing us round and round and round.

I never remembered leaving. Life would simply resume as normal at home. Dad would return to the University and his students, Mum would organise her charities, Finn would immerse himself in his music, I'd fill my diary with homework and friends. Granny, the cousins and Fairlights would all be held in stasis in my memory until the next end of term and release.

It's funny how things turn out. I was born in Ireland, where Dad was a professor of History at the time, and I was brought up in London after we moved there. I've worked all over the country since then, but my love for Fairlights has never faded. Even when the stock market crashed, taking Granny's income with it. Even when the cousins strode off to their own destinies and Granny had to convert paintings, china and all the Sheraton furniture into a pension trust. I still headed for Fairlights every holiday, I still loved it, I still needed that time apart. I went alone, sometimes with Finn, often with my best friend Annabel. We travelled by train, by National Express, once — God help us — hitchhiking (in retrospect, we deserved every word of the several rants delivered to us from on high for that escapade). Latterly we drove, the cars becoming less dilapidated and more reliable the older we got.

But I always visited, however briefly. I couldn't not go, whatever mess my personal life was in (which it frequently was), however busy I was at work. While I was there I'd drop into the County Records Office to log in any new Fairlights material that Dad had found, or just to leaf through the family archives. And then, with my head full of history, the ghostly, deserted rooms overlooking the sea would become even more of a canvas for my imagination.

There has only ever been one part of Fairlights that I avoid: the medieval open circular stair built into the back corner of the pele. It isn't used now, thank goodness — later ancestors had the sense to build a basic, conventional staircase at the front of the tower — but it still twists through every floor, a cold stone death trap giving me horrible shivers each time I pass one of its locked doors.

Recently, though, Granny has been the concern, living alone at Fairlights, refusing to move to somewhere smaller, warmer, more convenient and cheaper.

'I can't,' she'd say whenever the subject came up. 'Not yet.'

My mother tutted, worried about hips and ladders, falls and potential TIAs with none of us nearby to help. My cousin Tristram griped, citing the drain on the estate by Fairlights' extortionate maintenance costs (though I think, myself, he was more influenced by the promise of the high land prices routinely commanded by sought-after locations). Granny, however, was unbudge-able.

The thing is, even though I was also anxious about her, when I thought of Granny, I thought of Fairlights. Each was unimaginable without the other. Which is what gave me the courage to put a really scary fantasy of mine into action.

'Don't you start, Sorcha,' said Granny when I rang to cautiously sound her out. 'I've just had your eldest cousin on at me again about selling up. I can't think why. Your grandfather left Fairlights to me, not to his sons, and certainly not to any grandsons they might produce.'

'Tristram doesn't have a non-financial bone in his body,' I replied. 'Also, he's a bully. He's hoping to skim off a nice commission when he sells the land for you. Forget him. My idea is different and it involves *me*. Listen . . . '

Granny loved it.

'You're doing what?' shrieked Annabel when I told her.

I took a deep breath and repeated what I'd said. I was hoping that if I kept saying it out loud, it would stop sounding so fraught with disaster. 'I'm going to turn the Regency wing of Fairlights into a country house hotel, with luxury suites in the pele tower. The farmhouse stays private for Granny and me and the family.'

There was a small, awed silence. 'With your own money?'

'With kind of my own money. I'll have to borrow. Granny and I are forming a company. Some of the family are buying shares.'

'Sorcha Ravell, you are stark, staring bonkers. Do you want a chef? You do, don't you? You know you do. You do, you do, you do. I'll buy a stake. How much is a share and where do I send the cheque?'

* * *

The preliminaries were over. The die was cast. It was a golden day at the end

10

of September and I felt an exhilarating apprehension as the tower crenellations came into view on this, my first day home for good.

I've managed hotels all over the country. I've watched the growth in boutique getaways: quirky, individual places with good food, high standards of client care and every room different. I know I can make Fairlights profitable. There's plenty of leisure activity nearby, Annabel is a fabulous chef, and I've recruited local builders and craftsmen to recreate each of Fairlights' different eras in the neglected rooms. It is going to be completely glorious.

At the moment, though, it was still a terrifying mixture of my proposal and management skills, an account with the nearest building supplier, Tristram's venture capital, and a great deal of hard work.

I drove through the gates, running through the programme in my head — and nearly stalled in astonishment at the collection of dusty vans and last-legs estate cars on the driveway. Had I lost a day? Why was my workforce here already? I parked hastily and got out to see what was going on.

A number of faces I nearly recognised from the past formed a group on one side of the drive. On the other side were two faces I definitely knew, and they belonged to two people who shouldn't even have been here. Just what were my London-based cousin Tristram and his pet architect doing at Fairlights?

I stood for a moment, business instincts reasserting themselves. I wasn't rushing in before I'd assessed the situation. A tall man in a sea-grey t-shirt, as dark-haired as Tristram was fair, flung furiously away from my cousin, evidently ready to walk out before the job had even begun. He forged through the onlookers with a set face, and clashed arms with me when I wasn't quick enough to move out of the way.

He was in such a filthy temper, I doubt he'd have even broken step had he not seen I was female. Possibly my dark blonde hair and short skirt cut through the red mist in front of his eyes. He glanced at me irritably, then looked again. 'Oh, *now* you arrive,' he said.

Precognition doesn't strike me very often, for which I am extremely grateful. When it does, it is fierce and overwhelming and it invariably leaves me reeling. I could have done without it today. To be precise, I could have done without it at the exact moment when my shoulder clashed with his upper arm. Because despite his furious movements and sarcastic tone, foreknowledge of what this man and I would one day become streaked devastatingly right there and then up my spine. It rendered me powerless. It rendered me breathless and watery of limb. It was so strong, and brought with it such passion, that it was a wonder I could talk at all.

'Hi,' I managed. 'It's Nick Marten, isn't it? I wasn't expecting you today.' My eyes strayed to the rest of the scene. 'Or indeed any of this,' I added faintly.

Nick Marten — the man I'd

employed as foreman for the Fairlights conversion on the strength of his impressive CV, rather than him being the Whitcliff stone-skimming champion back when we were both fourteen and who I had *no idea* would have grown up quite this gorgeous — folded his arms and glared at me. 'I knew taking this job was a mistake. What sort of project manager calls people in when there's nothing ready?'

I'd got my second wind now. In a weird way, his tightly-focussed, blazing anger fed straight into my determination to get the building work done properly, even if it ruined me. 'One who's been pre-empted,' I replied.

I flipped open my handbag mirror and gave my hair a quick rake through with my fingers. Then I brushed down the front of my jacket and straightened my skirt. Arguing was always easier if one looked good. I walked through the local men, regretting my lack of heels as I'd been driving, and came to a halt in front of my cousin. 'Tris,' I said, kissing his cheek in cool greeting. 'What a nice surprise. Welcoming me to Fairlights just like in the old days. I wasn't expecting you.'

I should have remembered this thing about Tris. He is very hands-on and he doesn't like waiting. He really, *really* doesn't like waiting. He says that's how he made his money, grabbing slices of the action while his dragon pals were still considering long and hard before committing. His wife Erin is of the opinion that he might have a lot more disposable income if he *did* wait a little longer on occasion. Then again, if he'd waited that very first time she came on holiday to Whitcliff as a bored teenager, they wouldn't have had to get married in quite such a hurry and she wouldn't be in any position now to comment, would she?

'Sorcha,' he said, spreading his arms expansively. 'I thought I'd make a start. Alastair's raring to go.'

Alastair was Tristram's pet architect. His name on a set of plans was, apparently, all that was needed to get planning permission granted by any local council in the country. It was a confounded nuisance that he couldn't seem to limit himself to simply autographing them.

None of this showed on my face, but neither did any hint of conciliation. I'd never taken orders from Tristram yet and I wasn't about to start now. 'Same old Tris,' I said, maintaining my easy smile, 'I told you I was *arriving* today, not that we were starting work today. I only wound up my job at the Grand at the weekend. As it is, none of the materials are being delivered until tomorrow and we're having a full team briefing in the morning to walk through the whole project first. I assume you and Alastair would like to sit in?'

And with any luck that would be an end to their involvement. They'd realise I was making a good, professional job of this and they could go back to London in the knowledge that I wasn't wasting Tris's money. He could then hassle for results on one of his many other projects, letting me get on with Fairlights unmolested.

I waited, amused and smiling, ball in his court.

There was silence, broken only by the slap of the incoming tide on the rocks down below. Tris folded his arms. 'So what am I supposed to do today?'

Was there a hint of belligerent teenage sulk there? I pushed down a flash of triumph that I'd won. Things were never that simple with Tris. I raised my eyebrows. 'Our shiny new broadband is all set up and ready to go. Don't you have any financial wheeling and dealing to do?'

Alastair cleared his throat and spoke for the first time. 'Your change-of-use application for the hotel mentioned a sea angling business in the area . . . ' There was the smallest fanatical gleam in his eye.

Ah, so that was why Alastair was here. The lure of the wild, even though you'd never think it to look at him. I was hoping for other guests of a similar disposition to fill my expensive period bedrooms in the months to come. I gave my most proficient hotel-manager smile. 'Certainly there is. I'll find out if the skipper is free. You should have mentioned it was an interest of yours, Alastair. I could have set it up ready if I'd known you were coming. Just a moment.'

I crossed back to Nick, who had not after all gone. He had the air of watching the floor show just waiting for me to come a cropper. His very blue eyes were half wary, half grudgingly admiring. I'd have felt more comfortable if I'd known why he should be either of those things. 'Grown up, haven't you?' he murmured.

Now was not the time to respond in kind. Nick Marten might have dark, brooding, Celtic good looks, his t-shirt might show off builder's muscles and a summer tan, he might have his thumb hooked into the hip pocket of his denims like every teenage girl's favourite fantasy poster ever, but I needed to keep things on a professional footing between us for as long as possible for the sake of the project. I absolutely could not afford to be distracted.

It wouldn't last. I knew that for a certainty. My flashes of foreknowledge were exactly that. Knowledge. True premonitions. Not things that *might* come to pass, things that really would. 'But if you know what's going to happen, you can stop it,' Annabel had protested, many years ago. I remember she was making puff pastry at the time. I'd watched the dough slap onto the marble worktop and wondered how I could ever explain something so ephemeral to someone so essentially practical.

'That's just it. I can't,' I'd replied. 'It really will happen. What I *can* do is be prepared for the fallout afterwards.'

'It was all a misunderstanding,' I said to Nick Marten now. 'My cousin getting ahead of himself. Could you apologise for me, please, and let everyone know the briefing will go ahead in the morning as planned? They'll get half a day's pay for today.' And that would go straight onto Tristram's account, not mine.

He turned his head. 'Crossed wires,' he called. 'Eight-thirty tomorrow and bring your pack-ups.' He looked back at me, his dark blue eyes enigmatic. It was as if he was waiting for me to make some sort of comment. I only wished I knew what. Or why.

'Your brother-in-law,' I said briskly. 'The one with the sea angling boat. Do you know if he's free today? I have an architect in need of distraction.'

A tiny pause, then Nick flicked a glance past my shoulder. 'Your cousin too, I should imagine,' he said drily as he pulled a phone out of his pocket. 'I never thought to see him back again, I tell you.'

There was that edge of dislike again. Did they have history? Was that why Nick had been wary of accepting the job? Had Tristram stolen his girl some time in the past, perhaps? It would be like him.

'I never thought to be back myself

like this,' I said. Then I grinned, unable to keep the joy in. 'But I'm glad I am. It's going to be splendid, don't you think?'

His eyes widened in surprise. Good. We were going to be working closely together. I wanted him to know right from the start that I was doing this for me and Granny and Fairlights, not for profit. Well, not yet.

'Donal?' he said into his mobile. 'Do you want a charter today? The tide's about right. Two people, for as long as you like.' He listened and nodded, then strode over to Alastair and Tristram. 'The boat will meet you at the jetty in the harbour, gentlemen. The *Kathryn May*. All the gear you'll need is on board. Cash or card are equally acceptable. Enjoy your day.' He raised his hand in an ironic salute, turned smoothly, slanted me one more unreadable look and left.

2

Granny was baking. I dropped my holdall inside the door and inhaled deeply, filling myself with the essence of Fairlights. Right from my earliest memories, Granny's cooking has always seemed to me to be part of the fabric of the house. I don't ever remember the fridge without all the components of a full breakfast in it, the freezer bare of pies, or an empty cake tin on the dresser. I swear bringing Annabel here for the whole of one long, very wet summer when we were sixteen was what set her feet on the path towards becoming the top chef she is today. It was just so appropriate that she'd be joining me to run the hotel kitchen.

Granny's eyes lit up when she saw me. 'Hello, Sorcha darling, your room is ready. Oh, I am looking forward to this, aren't you? Steak and kidney pie tonight.' She was chopping sage. The aroma wafted upwards, sharp and green.

'Lovely. Hello, Granny.' I kissed the top of her head. 'Tristram and Alastair have gone out in Donal's boat, so you might need a quick change of menu if they're successful. Are they staying long, by the way? Have they said? I wish I'd known Tris was going to be here. I'd have been better prepared.'

'Fishing?' Granny's knife faltered.

Oh, how stupid of me, springing that on her without warning. I hugged her quickly, stooping to wrap my arms around her suddenly rigid body. My grandfather had been lost in a storm, long before I was born. Granny had been fearful of boats all the time I'd known her. 'It'll be fine,' I said. 'Donal's a good skipper. The *Kathryn May* is a stout boat. And it's a beautiful day — it's practically a millpond out there.'

She began chopping again, jerkily concentrated, sweeping the sage into an aromatic pile.

'I could kill for a cup of tea,' I said with casual cunning. 'And a piece of cake if there is one. I've been battling traffic the whole journey.'

That did it, she had the kettle on in a trice and a tin of brack out on the kitchen table, so stiff with fruit that a single slice could count as one of your five-a-day. Sad thoughts were buried in a flurry of domesticity.

'Heavenly,' I said, getting out plates and mugs. 'I shall put on pounds.'

'And then you'll worry them off,' said Granny drily.

I grinned. 'Starting with Tristram. He's already got the builders' backs up. That man has got no tact at all. How long is he staying and why are he and Alastair here anyway? Honestly, Granny, I could do without him right at the beginning like this. He's incapable of being idle and I'm going to have to fight him all the time to prevent him taking charge.'

'Row with Erin,' said Granny. 'I had her on the phone yesterday before he even arrived. Wanting to know when Annabel was moving in.'

'No! You're kidding.'

Granny shook her head.

'Oh, for goodness sake, that was *years* ago. She can't seriously believe he still fancies Annabel. It was Erin that he married and endowed with all his worldly goods, after all.' I paused. 'Actually, probably not *all* his worldly goods, knowing Tris.'

'Quite a lot of them, though,' said Granny. 'She'll have seen to that. Enough about him. How's your brother? I spoke to your father last week and he had no idea.'

'Yes, that's because Finn exists in the present, not hundreds of years in the past. Now if you'd asked Dad about the Border skirmishes between the Scots and the English way back when . . . '

Granny laughed. I told her Finn was well, on tour, and due to drop in towards the end of the year before heading for the studio to cut another album. 'It's not fixed though,' I said.

'You know Finn. If the muse takes him while he's here, we might have him all winter.'

'Ah well, at least he's cheap to feed. I've known birds eat more than your brother.'

'The trick is to catch him while he's concentrating on something else. Annabel once managed to get an entire week's stew into him by asking about the theme to his latest album while he was eating. He ate the whole pan without noticing.'

But all the time I was talking about Finn, I was wondering about my cousin. Erin might be paranoid where Tristram was concerned, but that didn't mean there *wasn't* a grain of truth to her suspicions. Blast the man. Surely he couldn't really still be hankering after Annabel? She wouldn't even be here for months, not until we were ready to open. Maybe it was just 'the one who got away' thoughts niggling at him. I'd have to warn her to be on her guard.

* * *

There were two ways of getting from Fairlights to the village. The conventional route by road, or the short-cut down the cliff steps to the beach. I've always loved walking along Whitcliff beach at dusk, so I went that way after supper this evening.

My feet moved down the stone steps with comforting familiarity, my hand on the rope rail recalled the millions of other times I'd slipped away at night like this. Then it had always been a holiday. Now I was properly home. Properly here to stay. Excitement bubbled beneath my ribs.

The wind was gentle at the bottom of the cliff, the smell of salt fresh in my nostrils. Under the soles of my shoes the surface of the sand was crisp. The tide was out. I could hear the sea whispering in the bay, lapping the strand, a reminder that it hadn't gone very far. I shut my eyes, wishing I could capture this moment in a sealed jar.

'You're back, then.'

I leapt, startled out of my thoughts, spinning to face the harsh voice. The speaker was young, younger than me anyway. I didn't recognise her. She was leaning against the cliff, a surly expression on her face in the last of the light. She had longish dark hair and wore narrow-fitting jeans and a thin bodice top. A long shawl-point cardigan was pulled tight around her slender frame. In an earlier era she'd have been smoking a cigarette. I could almost see a phantom thread of smoke coiling upwards.

'Yes,' I said, wary but pleasant. 'We're turning Fairlights into a hotel. It should bring some custom to the village.'

'About time too.' She continued to study me, on her face the unfriendliest expression I had ever seen in a local. 'You'd better not break his heart again,' she said venomously.

I stared at her, blood thrumming in my veins in shock. 'I'm not planning on breaking anybody's heart,' I stuttered.

'I'm here to run the hotel, that's all.' What was she talking about?

Her dark eyes narrowed to slits. Her voice was almost a hiss. 'Good, because I don't think he'd survive you a second time.'

This was insane. Who the hell was she? What was going on? Whatever it was, I wanted out of here fast. I nodded a rapid goodbye and hurried towards Whitcliff as quickly as the sand would let me, which wasn't very. The more I hurried, the more my feet sunk into the surface. Sand spurted in over the tops of my trainers. I could feel myself getting rattled, but didn't dare stop. When I finally rounded the cliff and looked back, she was still watching me from the shadows.

My legs felt clammy inside my jeans, my heart was pounding. That had been horrible. I emptied out my trainers and frantically cast my mind back, trying to recall her face. It was no use. If I'd ever known it, it was lost in past years. I started walking around the harbour,

jumpy now, skittering at every movement in the shadows. This was stupid!
My first evening back was being ruined
by a madwoman.

I wouldn't let it. I took a very long
breath, letting it go equally slowly.

*Focus, Sorcha. You know how to
deal with this. Look at what you're
seeing. Bring your emotions down a
level.*

Close-focus observation was a tech-
nique I made use of at work when I
needed to remain calm. If there was one
thing a hotel manager couldn't afford to
be in a crisis, it was flustered. Nor
could she burst into tears at the first
hint of trouble. I stood where I was,
counted to five, then walked on much
more slowly, noting all the changes
around Whitcliff harbour as I went.
There were a fair number. I came back
a lot, but in recent years the trips had
tended to be on the flying side, mostly
to see Granny, fitting in with work.
Even so, I'd returned far more often
than my cousins.

Now I made myself look around properly. There was fresh paint on a cottage, a garden gone to seed, new fishing nets, a bar instead of a shop.

I was breathing more easily, I could feel myself growing calmer, this was working. Good. Keep going.

The post office had a string of lights outside, the café had changed the colour of its curtains to a cheery orange, there was a different name on the restaurant next to the laundrette.

I was calmer still, and in addition, I'd noted several places of potential interest for my future visitors. The exercise was so successful, in fact, that my equilibrium had completely returned by the time I had walked the length of the curving harbour to the jetty at the far end.

I smiled at the sheer familiarity of this oldest part of Whitcliff, and reached out a hand automatically — as everyone in the village did — to stroke Grace.

Grace Ravell had been a very early

ancestress of mine. The carved wooden statue of her at this end of the harbour commemorated a phenomenal local event. Centuries ago, in the days when the Fairlight was still an open beacon, Grace Ravell had kept it going throughout a thirty-six hour hurricane when the whole of the Whitcliff fishing fleet had been trapped on the open sea by the storm. One by one, maintaining the Fairlight in a line above the Outer Light, the boats had struggled home. Not a single vessel or man had been lost.

The statue had been set here in her honour and almost immediately the fishermen started touching Grace for luck before casting off. Over time, the custom had spread to all Whitcliff inhabitants, sailors or no. Everyone had their favourite spot. It was noticeable that some parts of the statue were rather better polished than others.

My special place had always been Grace's left hand where it curled around the blazing torch. When I was younger, I'd had to scramble up the large piled stones at the base of the figure to reach it. Now I could stand on the plinth and just stretch to feel the slim hand under my palm, the wooden knuckles fitting into the hollows of my fingers.

I'd done it countless thousands of times to no ill effect, done it without even thinking about it. This evening should have been no different. But it was.

The moment I touched the smooth wood, the world around me rippled and I experienced the most horrendous dizzy, plunging sensation. I had to cling hard to the statue not to fall. *Trust me*, breathed a vibrant, musical voice in my ear, and I was petrified because I knew it was Grace speaking. Suddenly my feet were in her shoes and my hand was clenched on the hard iron torch holder. Blackness surrounded me, with just the flaring yellow light above my head casting sickening, whirling circles.

My knees buckled. I cried out,

breathless and nauseous. My foot slipped. I squeezed my eyes shut against the inevitable downward rush into an abyss of nothing.

I came to — surely only a second later — to the feeling of hands at my waist, trying to lift me down. My left palm was still clamped in a death grip around Grace's hand. 'I can't,' I slurred. Even my *teeth* ached. 'I can't move.'

'Dear God, what have I ever done to deserve this?' said an exasperated male voice.

The voice was like a stinging slap on my face. A solid body, smelling of damp Aran jumper, propped me against him while he prised my hand off the wooden statue. I came free from Grace in an inelegant rush, pins and needles in my feet, my cheek slithering against the roughness of the Aran sweater as I half-fell to the ground. I blinked open my eyes, still clutching at whoever had saved me, to find that a sea mist had rolled in.

'What the hell did you think you were doing?' The man's jumper wasn't the only thing that was rough. His voice was furious.

I looked at him dazedly, my heart-rate roughly three times what it should be. The two of us seemed to be islanded in the damp fog. I looked again. Dark hair. Very blue eyes. Nick Marten. It would be.

'I wasn't doing anything,' I said. 'I was saying hello to Grace, that's all.'

'You couldn't find an easier spot to touch? Just this once?'

'No! That's always been my place! I've never had a — ' I heard the words leaving my lips and just in time changed what I'd been about to blurt out. It wasn't everyone who could deal with precognition without slowly backing away and investigating contact details for the men in white coats. 'I've never got stuck like that before,' I said.

I stepped away from Nick, flexing my hands and feet, centring my emotions for the second time this evening.

He was still watching me. 'Damn good thing I came along. It would have been a great start to the building work at Fairlights — you with a leg in plaster.'

'It would take more than that to stop me,' I retorted.

He gave a short laugh. 'Is that so?' He glanced up at Grace. 'Why pick her hand, anyway? I've often wondered.'

He'd seen me do it before? More to the point, he'd remembered my spot from way back when we were teenagers? I was startled — and uneasy. Why would he remember that? We hadn't known each other particularly well back then. We'd just been two of the crowd. I shrugged, zipping up my fleece against the damp chill of the mist, zipping myself away from him, making a barrier. 'Why do any of us pick our places? It's always felt right. Besides — '

'Besides?'

What was it about Nick that made my tongue run on like this? I was extremely glad it was too dim for him to see the rising colour in my cheeks. 'My name — Sorcha — it means 'bringer of light' in Gaelic.' Although I hadn't known that until a lot later. I still recall the shiver that ran through me as I made the connection the first time I'd automatically reached for Grace's hand after I'd found out. 'Where do you touch?' I asked defensively.

'Are you serious?' He sounded incredulous.

There was a pause. I looked at him blankly.

When he spoke again his voice was bitter and distanced. 'All grown up was right,' he muttered. 'How stupid am I, eh?'

What had I said wrong? What were these undercurrents that I was unaware of? The air was certainly thick with something, though I honestly didn't know what or why. 'Thank you for steadying me,' I said. My voice came out clipped from being so confused. 'I was lucky you were there.' But why *was* he here?

'I was checking on the Outer Light,' he said, as if I'd spoken my last thought aloud.

Belatedly, I saw the line of wet footprints and the rowing boat tethered near the jetty steps. 'Isn't the buoy automatic?'

'It is, but the solar panel and the batteries still need maintenance. I'd rather not be manning the lifeboat the one time it decides to fail.'

Of course. He was a lifeboat volunteer. It had been on his CV. Tristram had grumbled about unreliability. I'd pointed out that four-fifths of the work force were volunteers and if there *was* a call-out, nothing would get done anyway since the boat in trouble would almost certainly belong to someone from the village. And when Tris said triumphantly that he'd told me all along it would be more cost effective to bring in a 'crack team from London', I countered with the fact that (a) our application had leaned heavily on our providing local employment, and (b) most of the crack teams in London were composed of builders from the north anyway, because there wasn't generally enough work for them up here.

It really was going to be so much less stressful when Tristram went home and left us alone.

Now I glanced up at Fairlights, rising half hidden from the mist. I should be getting back before Granny started worrying. Remembering the woman on the beach, I decided against returning by the cliff steps. 'Well, thanks again, Nick. I'll see you tomorrow,' I said, turning towards the road.

'Undoubtedly.' His arm half lifted towards me, then fell back by his side.

I felt his eyes on my back as the fog swallowed me. My thoughts chased each other in an uneasy jumble: the woman by the cliff, the sickening, darkness-and-flame whirling when I touched Grace's hand, Nick Marten being so familiar with me — yet so odd. Something was definitely going on that

I didn't understand.

I'd forgotten how quiet the village could be away from the waterfront. Inside the mist now, the silence was absolute, only my own footfalls to be heard.

I told myself I was calm. A sea mist was nothing new. Fuzzy globes of light from the roadside lamps marked the way up through the village for that very reason. I fastened my eyes on each one in turn, straining to hear anything over the damp, hollow sound of my footsteps. I was doing pretty well until the light ahead flickered and went out. Thick whiteness surrounded me, instantly robbing me of all directional sense.

And that's when I heard the sound of breathing behind me.

3

I stood absolutely still. The breathing was still behind me. And no matter how much I told myself that this was Whitcliff, for goodness sake, and when had anything *ever* happened here, the thick mist and deadened sounds added an edge of terror to all reasonable thought. As I failed to decide what to do, torchlight bloomed off to one side. I turned towards it thankfully.

'Sorcha?' called Nick Marten's voice.

Perversely, I was infuriated. I'd left him at the harbour! 'What are you doing up here?' I snapped into the whiteness. 'Were you following me?'

'Of course I was,' he replied, equally crossly. 'When I was prising you off Grace earlier, it was obvious you didn't have a torch about your person. Evidently I shouldn't have worried about you striding off blind into the fog.' He materialised next to me, turning the world manageable again.

'You could have said something! You nearly scared me to death.'

'It was pretty clear you wanted to be alone.'

'So you were stalking me for my own good?' Yes, yes, I know I was being childish, but he'd given me a shock.

'Look, I can take the torch away again . . . '

'No,' I said quickly. I drew a deep breath. 'Thank you. I'm . . . I'm sorry.'

We started off up the road again. I felt safer, walking through the fog with Nick, but no more comfortable. He seemed to thoroughly dislike me, so why had he followed in order to keep an eye on me? Come to that, why had he accepted the conversion work at Fairlights in the first place?

Again, as if he was reading my thoughts, he said, 'It was a good thing you turned up when you did this morning. I was ready to pay back the retainer and walk off the project. Your charming cousin was accusing me of incompetence because of nothing being in place.'

I would *kill* Tristram. 'I'm really sorry,' I said. 'Tris has always been impatient. It's his money funding the hotel conversion so he thinks he has the right to interfere. I should have gone with my instincts and borrowed from the bank, but this was quicker and there were fewer restrictions and . . . Oh well, hopefully he won't be around much. Why didn't you? Quit, I mean.'

'The usual. Bills to pay. It's an interesting project. I'm unlikely to find another long contract this close to home. And . . . ' He broke off.

After a moment when it was clear he wasn't going to continue, I said, 'I can see why being close to home is an attraction, but you must be used to having to travel for work at your level, surely? You've got an impressive CV, and there can't be that much period reconstruction going on around here.'

He shrugged. 'You'd be surprised.

But thanks. The point is, Ma isn't so good at the moment, so I prefer to be close at hand. Laurel was supposed to be keeping an eye on her in exchange for board and lodging, but she's now working all day, leaving Ma to look after the kid.'

I wrinkled my brow. 'Laurel?' Nick's CV hadn't mentioned a wife. If he was married, it was going to make my precognition *really* awkward. Although there was never any indication of how far in the future the incidents would actually happen, of course. It might be years yet (which thought depressed me a little, just showing how perverse I am).

'Yes, she split up from her bloke, so turned up here with Jamie. She always does. It won't last, and I get the feeling this time she'll light out leaving the boy behind.' Then, at my blank look, 'Laurel. My step-sister. You remember.'

No. No, I really didn't. Cold snaked from my belly to my shoulder blades. The way he'd said it, I *should* have known about her. Was it him winding me up? Or me really not knowing? I was getting such a bad feeling about this. 'Nick,' I said, swallowing. 'I don't — '

'Wait.' He raised a hand, listening, then turned. 'Who's there?'

Apprehension curled around me with the mist. If he thought we weren't alone as well, then I *hadn't* been imagining the menace earlier. I stood completely still and listened. Yes. The silence was full of someone else. Someone who wasn't Nick or me. Someone as immobile as we were.

Nick swore under his breath. 'Come on,' he said, taking my arm. He set off towards Fairlights twice as fast as we'd been going before.

'Do you know who it is?' I panted.

'I have my suspicions.' His voice was grim. 'Are you telling me you don't?'

There he went again. What did I not know, for goodness sake?

He misinterpreted my silence. 'Sorcha!' he said, making a frustrated movement.

'We can't keep ignoring this.'

Injustice swept through me. I wasn't ignoring anything! I was groping in the dark without a clue as to whether there was even a light switch or not! I opened my mouth to say as much, but we'd reached the top of the road and the Fairlights gateway had appeared insubstantially through the thinning mist. I heard the door to the house open, a faint oblong of light showed further off and Granny called, 'Sorcha? Is that you?'

'Coming,' I shouted back reassuringly. We walked towards the light. I felt jumpy and on edge, still emotionally wrung after the terrifying precognition at Grace's statue, very confused over Nick, and nettled because I didn't understand anything. All I wanted was to retreat to my room for an hour with a pot of tea and a book and put the whole world out of my head.

Nick, however, was continuing his intense simmering beside me. I wilted at the thought of sorting it out tonight, but bottled emotion was likely to go off at any time, taking out everything in its path, and for reasons I didn't quite follow, I couldn't simply leave him. Besides, there was that other foreknowledge regarding him. It would be a disaster to set that train of events off too soon.

I stopped at the veranda. 'Thanks for seeing me back, Nick,' I said. 'You were right, I'd forgotten about the mist. Stupid of me. Look, I'm really tired and we're going to be working together on this conversion for months. Can we start again and just act like normal professionals, do you think?'

He was as motionless as though I'd dunked him in ice. His face was unreadable. 'Fine. As you wish. My pleasure. I'll see you tomorrow — boss.' And he strode off in the direction of the cliff steps to be swallowed by the mist.

Well done, Sorcha. That went splendidly. Not.

★ ★ ★

'We have a problem.'

I looked up to see Nick in the doorway of my office. 'Another one?' I asked, bracing myself. 'What is it this time?'

At least it wouldn't be Tristram rubbing Nick up the wrong way again. He'd gone off at last to hound some other part of his empire that wasn't delivering fast enough. About time too. I swear he'd been at Fairlights more this past fortnight than in the five *years* beforehand. It wouldn't bother me if he never came back.

As always in Nick's presence, I was aware of every single thing I was wearing. Whether it revealed too much or not enough. Whether it was too long, too short, too dressy, too casual. I was cross with myself, because I usually assembled working outfits easily. Partly it was the fault of the terrain. I had hotel-manager clothes in plenty, but it wouldn't be appropriate to wear pencil skirts, for example, while I was walking around what was effectively a building site. On the other hand, I was managing this project, so it wouldn't do to dress sloppily either. I'd settled by teaming smart jeans with a selection of crisp blouses, and either boxy jackets or long cardigans on top. Occasionally I added a statement necklace to keep people on their toes. And lipstick.

Nick, naturally, looked devastating in whatever he wore. Today it was a soft blue denim shirt and ancient grey cargos. To be honest, I wasn't so much bracing myself to deal whatever problem he was about to raise, as bracing myself to keep a professional distance from the man himself. Since the encounter by the jetty that first evening we'd been circling each other like wary cats. It was odd, Nick couldn't know about my foreknowledge, but he was clearly as aware of me as I was of him. And it was more than just mutual attraction, though there was bagloads of that. No, I couldn't shake the feeling that there was a twisting sword of something else in the air, something I didn't know about.

All in all, it didn't make for the easiest of partnerships. I had the sensation of working on borrowed time, and Nick gave the impression of primed dynamite about to blow up. That this wasn't his normal demeanour was evident from the joking remarks of his colleagues.

'Your architect — ' he said now.

'My cousin's architect, not mine.' I didn't want Nick equating us. Tristram was only in this for the money and the power. I was doing it for love.

Nick shrugged, apparently unbothered by the distinction, which annoyed me even more. 'If you say so. Anyway, Alastair has had the visionary idea of losing the Fairlight. He says the cupola will make a lovely viewing platform for the guests without the lantern in the way. Once we've shifted it six foot or so.'

I shot to my feet. '*He what?* But the Fairlight is part of Whitcliff. It might be needed any day!'

'Are you going to tell him, or shall I?'

I narrowed my eyes. 'Is that a rhetorical question?'

'I'll hold your coat,' offered Nick, deadpan.

For a moment, it was almost as if we were having a normal conversation. I felt a pang of something lost, and shook my head to clear it. 'Where is he?' I asked.

'Physically? On the tower roof, at one with the view.'

I reached for a lightweight padded jacket. It would be chilly up there. Not that it was exactly warm here in my office. I was hoping that by winter we might not have to have *all* the external doors open all of the time. I said as much now to Nick as a joke.

'You could always try doing up another button,' he muttered, looking out of the courtyard window.

I stared at his averted profile in amazement. That had come out in a remarkably sorely-tried voice. Then I swivelled hastily as his head started to turn. 'It's an open neck blouse,' I said with an attempt at tartness. 'It's supposed to look like this. Come on. We'll go through the house.'

Instead of going outside via the veranda, I exercised family rights and took Nick down the service passage leading from the back of my office — which had been the butler's pantry in Regency and Victorian times — past the storerooms and 'domestic offices' straight through to the farmhouse kitchen. Granny pressed home-made biscuits on us as we passed. Nick took one, flushed with surprised pleasure. A disconcerting glimpse of him younger tugged at my memory, looking exactly like that, even to the biscuit in his hand.

'Seems odd, having the run of the place,' he said through a mouthful of chocolate-chip. 'In the old days I wouldn't have been allowed anywhere near.'

'That's not true,' I said. 'The crowd often came here.' I recalled long evenings in the music room, the late sun lying in patterns across people's faces, drinking cola, eating cake and sausage rolls, listening to everybody's CDs.

He snorted. 'You think? Once a holiday, maybe twice during the summer. And not me, latterly. Your cousin would have seen to that.' He sent me an enigmatic glance as he brushed crumbs off his fingers into the sink, plainly expecting me to understand.

I felt a shaft of unease. This sort of thing still kept happening and it was edging me towards screaming point. It was as if I was locked outside a world that everyone else had access to. Why? What did they know that I didn't? The trouble was, every time it happened, it got that little bit harder to ask.

★   ★   ★

The pele tower was old and solid. It breathed history and exuded a massive, medieval safety. It would, I hoped, appeal to those people looking for a different sort

53

of holiday accommodation. There would be suites on all five floors. The stately Edwardian lift — thankfully installed long before the historical busybodies tried to get the tower listed — would convey guests up and down in magnificent retro style and Alastair's clever lighting would make up for the small defensive windows. I was already drafting lavish, atmospheric copy for the hotel brochure and website.

Visitors and builders used the outer veranda door to get into the pele, but the internal family entrance was at the far right-hand corner of the kitchen where the Georgian farmhouse butted onto the rear wall of the tower. According to the archives, breaking through the four-foot-thick wall had taken several days back in the 17th century. It had resulted in a short incongruous tunnel leading between the kitchen and the pele. In my view, they hadn't helped matters at all by fitting arched Gothic doors at each end. The Stuart version of B&Q had probably had them lying around for years waiting for a suitably suscep-tible client. I took a deep breath as we walked through the narrow passage, very much aware of the pele stair on the other side of the wall.

In the tower I turned quickly right, towards the lift, but Nick slowed to a dawdle. 'I haven't been down this end before,' he said, looking to the left with interest. 'Is that the doorway to the original pele stair?'

'Yes.' Despite my best intentions my voice came out cracked. 'It's not safe. We never use it. It's kept locked.'

'How do you mean, not safe? Crumbling? Rusting?'

'The design,' I said rapidly. 'The design is dangerous. It's an open stone cylinder, with a rope handrail and anticlockwise steps built directly into the wall. There's nothing in the centre. Nothing at all. Really nothing. Empty air. Sheer drop if you miss your footing.'

He looked at me quizzically. 'You don't like it?'

'It bloody terrifies me,' I said.

'Fair enough. Who has the key? We're going to be working up and down the pele. I really ought to have a look at this stair so I know what I'm forbidding the guys to use.'

A heartbeat passed, during which I heard the thump of blood in my ears. I drew the ring of Fairlights keys shakily out of my bag, fitted the long iron barrel into the lock and turned it with a resistant thunk. My fingers were trembling so much I had to force them not to slither off the cold metal. With apprehension coiled tight in my stomach, I grasped the handle and pulled open the squat, black-painted door.

I don't know what I was expecting. My terror of the pele stair had gone beyond rational thought. Absurdly, my first reaction as the door opened was one of pure surprise. The circular stair shaft held an innocuous pearly dimness instead of the groping dark I remembered. A faint light picked up glints in the pinkish sandstone, indicating the presence of window slits further up. I pictured the outside of the pele tower and realised that *of course* this corner had windows. So why had I remembered the stair as devil black all these years?

As I stood there, bewilderment rooting me to the spot, I breathed in ancient stone and old dust mixed with the sweeter air from outside. That was another anomaly. In my memory there was salt — and a choking paraffin smell. I have never been so puzzled in my life.

Nick squeezed past me through the doorway and straight away tipped his head back to look upwards. 'Hmmm,' he said, 'I see what you mean about the drop. Interesting construction, though.' He put his foot on the first step.

My terror rushed back. 'I hope your insurance is up to date,' I said, a tremor in my voice.

He glanced at me. 'Come off it, Sorcha. This stair is no worse than the cliff steps and I've seen you run up and down *them* hundreds of times. Same rope handrail against the wall. Same sheer drop the other. And the cliff top is higher than this.'

I blinked. I looked at the stone steps, built into the circular wall. My heart gave an enormous thump of shock. He was right. I was so stunned that I missed the reference to 'hundreds of times'. Then my ears caught up with his words.

When? When had he seen me coming down the cliff steps hundreds of times? 'I get claustrophobic,' I said feebly, not really concentrating on what I was saying.

'Oh, like Laurel. Whenever the family has a day on Donal's boat she has to stay on deck instead of going into the cabin.'

There he went, mentioning Laurel again as if I knew her. And I still didn't. His older sister Kathryn I remembered perfectly well, but not Laurel. Together with my utter confusion over the pele stair, I wasn't sure I could take much more of this.

Nick, however, was unaware of my

state of mind. He studied the doorway with a tiny frown. 'Why did they build this so narrow? It must make it almost impossible to carry furniture up and down.'

'We use the lift,' I muttered, and before he could tell me that he meant in the old days, I went on, 'The records say they took stuff up in sections for assembly in the rooms. You're forgetting the original purpose of the pele. The stair doors are the width of a human body for defence.'

I followed him gingerly into the stone stairwell to show him what I meant. 'When it was just a fortified tower, without the farmhouse or anything, down here was the undercroft. Whenever danger threatened, the livestock would be driven inside, the family would retreat upstairs and both doors would be barred.' I pointed to the iron brackets either side of the inner doorway. 'In those days, this stair was the only entrance to the upper levels. That meant attackers couldn't pour in — and because the outer door is on the seaward side there wasn't the space for marauders to mass outside. Archers could fire down from the roof and the fighters of the family would wait inside to pick off the enemy one at a time.' I gestured up at the stairs. 'That's why the steps are in an anticlockwise spiral. Most people are right-handed. Even if they did get in, anyone going up has their sword hand against the wall, whereas the family coming downwards have their fighting arms free.'

Nick was already climbing the open stair. I jiggled uneasily, watching him, and bit off a small shriek as he turned and made a mock parry coming down the spiral. Then he repeated it going upwards. 'So they would,' he said. 'How clever. Not sure I'd want to test it out for real. I suppose it's different when you're fighting for your wife and children. Anything would take second place to keeping them safe. Presumably that's why there's no central pillar?'

'Yes. Nick, would you please come down now?'

He raised his eyebrows and descended, sure-footed and subtly powerful. Even through my deep distrust of the stair, the thought came to me that he would have been a very reassuring person to have on your side, back in the old days.

'I didn't know you cared,' he said. Then, looking at me more seriously as he joined me in the passage, 'This stair really does give you a bad time, doesn't it?'

'Nothing gets by you.' I locked the door behind us with rather more force than was necessary.

There was a heartbeat's silence as he studied me. 'How about the upper doors? Are they secure too?'

I nodded and headed for the lift with a lot more speed than I'd made when dragging my feet towards the pele stair. 'Oh yes. There are locked, metal grilles pulled across on the inside, and the outer doors are locked too. That should keep the safety inspectors happy.'

Nick sauntered after me. 'I must say I do like the pele as a defensive structure.

Were there many attacks?'

'Heavens, yes, the early family records are full of them. They were all written by men, so the battles are recorded in an excess of loving detail. I often thought, if it had been the Fairlights women writing them up, there would have been rather more in the way of how long things took to clean up afterwards and how they managed to cater for a siege.'

At this, Nick laughed out loud, surprising me. Except that in an odd way it didn't surprise me at all.

'Where are they kept? The records?'

'The family archive is in the County Records Office now. It *was* at Fairlights — one of the pele rooms was used as the library for years — but what with having to sell all the valuables for Granny's trust fund, and Dad being the only one of his generation to really be interested in the history, he suggested to the family that he would index it and so forth, but that the county should look after the archive for us, in return for making the material available to researchers. They jumped at the opportunity, of course. It's the most complete family record they have. So now, every time Dad comes across something new, one of us takes it over there and they add it.'

The lift mechanism rumbled. A couple of seconds later, the heavy Edwardian door slid sideways with the slow ponderous grandeur of an earlier age. I stepped into the warm, wood-lined interior with a smile. I did love this lift. I pressed the top button and noticed Nick watching me, a very strange look on his face.

'What is it?' I asked.

He shook his head. 'Nothing. How often is the lift serviced?'

And we talked maintenance contracts for the rest of the trip to the roof.

4

Alastair was standing between two of the crenellations, gazing out to sea. 'I adore this view,' he declared. 'Just look at those lines, at the power of the landscape. I've decided I'd like to book the top pele suite permanently.'

'Being an architect pays that much?' I asked.

Behind me I heard Nick smother a laugh.

Alastair looked puzzled, then turned to Nick. 'Is this a west wind? Donal said the fish run better in a westerly down this coast, but I don't know whether he means the wind blows *from* the west or *to* the west.'

'From,' said Nick. 'And a westerly is all very well, but if it turns from a wind into a gale you've got trouble.'

'Which is why you can't remove the Fairlight,' I said, coming to the crux of the matter.

Alastair smiled in the intensely patronising way architects have. 'The cupola is unsafe, I'm afraid. I know, I know. I'm frantic about it as a feature, but the walls need bracing. And look at it, it's in completely the wrong place, set back there.'

I gritted my teeth. 'On the contrary, it is in completely the *right* place. The Fairlight has been the top leading light for guiding boats into Whitcliff harbour for centuries. I'm not exaggerating, Alastair. Centuries. It *has* to be exactly where it is. If you don't believe me, I'll take you out in the rowing boat and show you. By starting out at sea with the Outer Light off to port, and then steering to bring the two lights into line, vessels put themselves on the right approach for the harbour without any danger of being holed on the rocks. You can't remove the lantern *or* shift its position.'

I might just as well not have spoken. The look of pitying superiority remained on his face. 'But, Sorcha, the lantern isn't used,' he pointed out gently, as if to one with weak intellect.

I reminded myself that Alastair knew nothing of Whitcliff. 'Not on a daily basis any more, no, but it has to be ready and functional in case of an emergency. The women of the Ravell house have always had a duty to maintain the Fairlight in good working order. Originally the beacon was wood chips in a brazier, now it's an oil lantern with a Fresnel lens. Grace Ravell — whose statue is down at the harbour — kept the light going single-handed through the worst storm in Whitcliff's history. You are *not* moving it.'

Nick was standing in the lee of the cupola, hands in the pockets of his cargos, enjoying my tirade. 'And I guarantee if you ask the guys to try, they'll walk out. I don't think there's a family in the village without a connection to the sea.'

Alastair looked from Nick to me as if unable to believe we were serious. 'I'll text Tristram,' he said, and walked in a dignified fashion to the lift.

Nick chuckled. 'He's going to be disappointed. Even your cousin knows the value of the Fairlight. Let's see this ever-ready lantern of yours, then.'

I gave him a filthy look. 'Thank you. I'm so glad you waited to ask that until *after* he'd gone. Granny hates heights — she can't cope with them at all. I cleaned the lantern and the spares a couple of months ago, so they will be serviceable, but I suspect they could do with some tender loving care again.'

Nick followed me up the three steps into the cupola, watching with interest as I lifted down the lantern and unlatched the nearest bench seat to get out a spare and the cleaning materials. 'What's its range?' he asked.

'Nine miles, I think. I haven't been out that far to check for myself.'

He swivelled slowly, gazing through the windows, over the crenellations, to where white tops of waves frothed the grey-green water and raced each other towards land. 'Alastair's got a point, you know — this would make a fantastic viewing platform.' A gust of wind made the wooden walls of the cupola creak. 'And he's right about that too. It needs attention.'

'Hotel first, extras later,' I said firmly. 'The cupola is just a fancy shelter, when all's said and done. The Fairlight doesn't need it in order to work.'

★ ★ ★

I rang Annabel next day to find out when it would be convenient for her to come and specify kitchen equipment. 'We need to know the plumbing runs too — where you want the sink and so forth. I can pick you up at Carlisle station if you don't want to drive.'

'Oooh, sold,' she said on a great gusty sigh. 'Then I can sleep on the train. It's going to be madness here this weekend. The cretinous sales team have booked us to cater three weddings in five hours, would you believe! But I'm free Monday and I reckon they owe me a few days off. How is everyone? Has Finn arrived yet? I can't tell you how much I'm longing for it all to be ready so that I can get up there for good. Not that they know anything about that *here* just yet.'

I grinned down the phone. 'Finn's not coming until Christmas, and yes, I'm rather looking forward to everything being ready myself. We're fine. Granny and I were feeling a bit outnumbered with all the testosterone striding around the place and clashing antlers, but Tristram has gone off to bring some of his other projects up to the mark, so it's much quieter. Apparently things don't happen by themselves.'

Annabel laughed. 'Really? I bet *you're* getting on better without him.'

'You're not kidding. Or rather, we would be if he hadn't left Alastair-the-architect here to be his eyes and ears.'

'This is the same Alastair who is useless at the day-to-day stuff, is it?'

'That's the one. Unfortunately, according to my foreman, he doesn't know enough to realise it.'

'I had a restaurant manager like that once. Shall I vamp him while I'm up there and get him out of your hair?'

'I should think he'd run a mile. Besides, he's talking about renting the top pele suite semi-permanently so you'd have all that awkward, letting-him-down-gently, it's-not-you-it's-me, of-course-I-still-respect-you bit to do afterwards. It's okay, I lost patience with him today and told him we wanted all the different rooms to be as authentic as possible on a limited budget, so could he look around and nab us a few bargains. He disappeared onto the Internet and I haven't seen him since.'

'You are a bad woman.'

'Takes one to know one.'

'Talking of which, I've got a sous-chef to put in his place this afternoon, so I'd better go. Ciao, sweetie.'

'Bye, hon. Text me when your train's due in.'

The prospect of seeing Annabel on Monday, and having beautifully normal conversations without stubbing my toe on hidden meanings everywhere, cheered me immensely. I declined nicely next morning when Alastair told me there was a viewing of a country house sale and asked if I'd like to go with him. I even bore it with equanimity when he returned at the end of the day with the light of a fanatic in his eye and an option in his hand on a 1920s closed stove that would be *perfect* for the hotel kitchen. I couldn't quite bring myself to sigh sympathetically, but I did manage a regretful tone when pointing out that coal ranges didn't sit at all well with speedy early breakfasts and Health & Safety in Kitchens directives. I also reminded him that Annabel — who had a full set of certificates herself — had her own budget for the kitchen and knew best how she worked and what she would need. 'It's my experience,' I added sagely, 'that crossing professional chefs is rarely worthwhile.'

Annabel hadn't been back to Fairlights for a couple of years and her enthusiasm for the transformation was just as I'd hoped. The far end of the ballroom itself, with its spectacular views over the sea and the gardens, was already taking shape as the restaurant. She was as excited as me as I explained which other rooms were turning into what, both of us waving our arms and talking at the same time. As a man, the builders (who treated *me* with the distant tolerance reserved by craftsmen for the person who paid them) were mesmerised by my spectacular friend with her bubbly chestnut curls and her vibrant yellow Fifties tea-dress. If we didn't leave a trail of bent nails and half-sawn pieces of timber in our wake, it was a miracle.

Nick, while not exactly mesmerised, accompanied us with open amusement. 'Why has she not been snapped up as a television cook?' he asked me as Annabel waltzed the room estimating table space.

'It's funny you should mention that,' I said. 'She *was* approached one time, but it turned out that she'd had a messy affair with the director the previous summer, so the TV company changed tack and went with some fourteen-year-old prodigy instead. The programme sunk without trace, I believe.'

'More fool them. Does she wear the frilly skirts to work?'

'Get real,' said Annabel, returning from twirling happily around her embryonic restaurant. 'Do you have any idea how much this dress costs to dry clean?'

'To business,' I said, and chivvied the pair of them through the swing door into the shell of Annabel's new kitchen, where she proceeded to startle Nick by becoming totally professional, lucid and — crucially — within budget.

'Are you one of these sweary, shouty chefs?' he asked after the major details had been sorted out. 'If so, we might have to do something about the sound-proofing in here. Can't have the diners upset.'

I gave him a long look. His tone

might be conversational, but I knew exactly why he'd said it. Annoyingly, Tristram had returned this morning — eyes everywhere for lack of progress — and had been talking continually since he'd arrived. He was on the phone next door now, in what had been the music room while we were growing up, the supper room in Regency days, and which (in a satisfying twist to me) would become the lounge bar in our incarnation.

Annabel frowned, listening to Tris threatening some poor unfortunate with withdrawal of funds if there weren't visible results soon. 'Didn't you tell me Nick was going to have that room as his office, Sorcha, before it gets knocked through? What's Tristram doing in there?'

'That was the original plan,' I replied, meeting Nick's eyes. 'But Tris decided he and Alastair needed the space and the light, so Nick is having to make do with the old card room. Silly me, I'd assumed once Alastair had drawn up the plans and Tris had transferred the dosh, their part would be over and they wouldn't need working space.'

And then I closed my mouth in a tight line, in case the hearing-through-walls worked both ways. I was still cross about it. The old card room was to the right of the front door, next to my office, and was due to become open-plan as the reception area of the hotel. Not the most congenial of working spaces for the foreman of a big project, with partitions coming down and being rebuilt all around him.

'More convenient for him organising the builders,' Tristram had said when I remonstrated.

'But they won't be able to talk over any grievances in private,' I pointed out.

Tristram had smoothed his faultless hair and replied in a cool voice that if the men had grievances, they might feel happier not working on the project at all. At which point I'd gone outside, reminded myself why I needed his dratted capital and stomped up and down the beach for a while until I could speak without spitting.

'I don't mind,' Nick said now, directly to me.

'Well, you bloody ought to,' I grumbled.

Nick went back to work, and Annabel and I returned to the farmhouse kitchen to have lunch with Granny. Tris and Alastair joined us a few minutes later. I made a mental note to top up Granny's housekeeping from the hotel account. I didn't see why she should keep providing our unasked-for consultants with free meals.

The lunch conversation was saved from being exclusively about Tristram's current projects by Erin ringing him half way through for a blazing row about his missing one of the kids' concerts tonight and her having to make his apologies *again* when he had *promised* he wouldn't let them down any more, and just when had they decided that a *bloody text message* while she was at the hairdresser was adequate warning that he was going to be away from the marital home for a week?

'The difficulty in these situations,' murmured Annabel into my ear, 'is always whether to pretend we haven't noticed the argument and make small talk between ourselves . . . or admit to the elephant in the room and fall tactfully silent.' She paused thoughtfully. 'In which case we might hear Erin too.'

'You could always ask Tris to press the loudspeaker button so we can listen properly,' I suggested.

Annabel let out a shriek of laughter. Immediately there was another furious explosion from the phone. Annabel has always had a very distinctive laugh.

Tristram's good-looking face took on a mulish expression. 'I *told* you I came up to see Alastair about the hotel conversion and *your* new conservatory. I didn't even know Annabel was going to be here. For God's sake, Erin, take a bloody video of Scarlett's concert. I'll watch it when I get back. Now if you'll excuse me, my lunch is getting cold.'

He shut the phone off and turned back to his plate. 'So,' he said. 'How much is this kitchen of yours going to cost me, Annabel?'

I smiled sweetly. 'It's going to cost *the hotel* exactly what we budgeted. That was lovely, Granny. Thank you. Do you want a hand with the washing up?'

* * *

After lunch, Annabel wanted to revisit former haunts. 'Tristram doesn't change, does he?' she said as we strolled down through the village towards the harbour. 'He always did want to be king of the coop. I'm glad I resisted his blandishments all those years ago. I prefer my men a lot more appreciative and much more restful.'

'Leon wasn't restful,' I objected, referring to her last boyfriend and their acrimonious split.

'No, but he was appreciative.' She

78

made a face. 'To begin with, anyway.'

I linked my arm in hers. 'Yeah, that's the trouble with food critics. They love every mouthful until they've been right through the menu, then they get bored.'

Annabel sighed. 'So true. Next time I go to the man store, I'll stipulate a leisurely, gentle, sensitive soul who just thinks I'm the most marvellous creature in existence.'

'That definitely rules Tris out,' I said. 'Not only is he convinced that *he* is the most marvellous creature in existence, he believes you should never put off until tomorrow what you can do right here, right now, at the top of your voice.'

'He certainly moved way too fast for me as a teenager. Good thing I kept saying no and he found Erin instead.'

I thought back to that long rainy summer when, in the narcissistic manner of sixteen-year-olds, Annabel and I were joined at the hip and far more concerned with ourselves and our troubles than we were with the outside world. This hadn't gone down at all well with Tristram, the tallest, blondest, best-looking and most uncomfortably restless of my cousins. He wasn't accustomed to being ignored.

'What always surprises me is that he and Erin are still together,' I said. 'I suppose with three children it would get a tad expensive to do anything else.'

'True,' said Annabel. 'At least having children is one mistake neither you nor I have ever made. I think we might have a full tally of the rest between us.'

'Ahem,' I said reprovingly. 'I believe Erin looks on Scarlett as a master stroke rather than a mistake.'

Annabel grinned. 'She could be right at that. How old was Tristram then? Twenty? Twenty-one? I can't see him even recognising her by the next holiday otherwise.' She hesitated, then slid a glance at me. 'Especially as I always thought the person he really wanted to get off with was you. The rest of us were just camouflage.'

I felt a jolt of surprise. 'Me? You're

kidding. He's my cousin. I never felt the slightest spark for any of my cousins.'

'Perhaps that was what attracted him. You were a challenge.'

'Now you're being silly. I saw them all every holiday, that's practically like growing up together.'

Annabel shrugged. 'I might have been imagining it. It's all water under the bridge now. I like Nick Marten, by the way. A man who gets on with his job efficiently and without fuss is a rare thing. And rather hunky with it. Those eyes. Mmm-mmm. Why was he never around when I was here?'

I squashed a tiny twinge of alarm that she was attracted to Nick and said, 'I don't know. I remember him from quite early on. He must have moved away. I know it took me a moment to place him when he applied. As soon as I saw his CV I emailed him a contract by return!'

'No love lost between him and Tristram, is there?'

She'd noticed it too, just on a morning's acquaintance. 'No, there isn't,' I said. 'Probably a girl, knowing Tris.' Though privately I thought any girl would need her head examining if she preferred my cousin to Nick Marten.

'Have you asked him? Nick, I mean. Not Tristram.'

I hesitated. 'No, I . . . he seems to think I ought to know.'

'Oh.' Annabel paused, and then gave a bright smile. 'Ah well, I daresay you'll find out.'

I knew that tone. 'What is it?' I asked in my best long-suffering voice. 'What idiot idea has come to roost in your head now?'

She gave me a sly peep. 'Got a little thing going on there, haven't you?'

She *didn't* want him for herself. I felt my face heat, ashamed of the relief. 'No,' I said. 'Absolutely not.'

She waited.

'Well, not yet,' I said, giving in.

'Thought so.' Annabel blew on her fingers in a satisfied manner and looked around the harbour. Her gaze alighted on the Whitcliff teashop. 'Fancy a cuppa?'

I laughed. 'Checking out the opposition?'

'I'm just thirsty, sweetie,' she said, radiating innocence.

We sat at a window table covered in cheerful orange gingham, and settled down to have a nice gossipy catch-up. 'This is such bliss,' I said. 'Honestly, I don't know what's got into — ' And then I stopped. To my horror, the angry woman from the beach on my first night home was marching over to us, order pad in hand, face like a thundercloud.

She glowered at me. 'You might as well get up and leave again right now. You won't find any staff here to poach.'

My hackles rose instantly. 'I'm not here to poach staff! That's not the way I do business. Besides, my friend here is going to be the chef at Fairlights, so she'll be the one interviewing. We've come in for a pot of tea, please.'

The malevolent gaze slewed towards

Annabel. 'You want to watch out,' she hissed. 'I'd rather slit my wrists than work for her after what she did. He's never been the same. Never. And still he goes back. He must be mental.' She turned on her heel and flounced towards the kitchen.

Annabel was round-eyed with shock. 'Crikey, Sorcha, what was all that about? What did you do to her?'

My heart was thudding. 'You tell me! I don't even know who she is!'

'Local madwoman, perhaps? I don't usually like the things, but there's an argument for staff wearing those cheery *'Hello, I'm Tim, I'll be your waiter today'* badges, isn't there?'

I gave a reluctant chuckle, but the encounter had disturbed me badly. Even alone here with Annabel, my problems were still lying in wait, all prepped to go for the jugular when I least expected it. 'Perhaps she's got me mixed up with someone else,' I said, playing it down.

Annabel looked at me shrewdly and

changed the subject.

The tea was slammed down on the table five minutes later as if we were contagious. Annabel said a beautifully polite thank you, asked if there might be any biscuits and we continued to discuss the colourful doings of her father's third wife and her mother's new toy boy. Even this wasn't easy with the hostile waitress staring out of the window not ten feet away.

'D'you know, I really don't think we need to worry about competition once we get the restaurant going, Sorcha,' murmured my friend under her breath. 'I've never seen a surer way of scaring off potential customers in my life. If any of my staff acted like this they'd be in the next county before they realised they'd been fired.'

The atmosphere was so inhospitable that we drank up rapidly. Annabel had just asked for the bill when there was a crash from the kitchen and the tea-room owner put her head around the kitchen door. 'Laurel,' she called.

The sullen waitress turned. 'Yes?'

'Can you run up to the shop and get me some eggs, pet? I've just knocked a whole box on the floor.'

The pit of my stomach dropped away. The orange and white squares of the tablecloth blazed a chequerboard across my vision as I gripped the table. The waitress was called Laurel? *She* was Nick's step-sister? There couldn't be two such names in the village, surely? So whatever it was she thought I had done — breaking '*his*' heart, letting '*him*' down — it must be Nick she thought I'd done it to! But how? And when? I had no memory of *anything* that might have caused such antagonism. No memory at all. My head spun. I felt so sick I barely made it outside.

'I don't like to say anything,' said Annabel mendaciously, once she had paid the bill and had joined me on the street, 'but you look as if you need a whole bottle of rescue remedy.'

I gazed at my friend, disbelief screaming and shouting inside me. 'I'm missing a chunk of memory, Annabel. I really am.' Even saying the words was crazy, like validating the impossible. How could this have happened? It felt as though the whole world was shaking to pieces around me. 'That waitress is Nick Marten's step-sister. Both of them apparently think we've met, but I barely remembered *him*, let alone know anything about her. I mean . . . ' I trailed off, then restarted despairingly. 'This sort of thing just doesn't happen. I don't even know when it is that I've lost.'

Annabel looked stricken. 'Oh, honey,' she said, letting her bag fall to the ground and wrapping her arms around me in a hug.

It was sturdy, uncritical friendship, and it was exactly what I wanted. I leant into her vital, vibrant warmth. 'Thank you,' I said shakily. 'You're a life saver.'

'By believing you? Come off it, Sorcha. Quite apart from all the times I've wept on your shoulder over the years, you saved my sanity when you brought me here that first summer after my parents broke up. It drew a line between my old life and the new one. Two whole months of time out.'

That was how I'd always thought of Fairlights too. Time out. Time apart. But something, some time, must have gone horribly, horribly wrong and I didn't know what — or when — it was.

'I'll tell you one thing for free,' said Annabel. 'I don't know either Nick or that Laurel at all, so whatever it is must have happened one year when I wasn't here.'

We talked about it all the way back to Fairlights, trying to narrow it down, but I simply wasn't aware of anything missing. Horror roared in my head. The vanished time was eating away at me, a solid lump of incredulity in my chest. The only thing I knew was that Nick Marten was heavily involved. I needed to find him. Fast.

5

Nick, when I rang his mobile, was on the top floor of the pele tower. 'I'm measuring up for the bathroom partition in here. I thought it might keep Alastair quiet if he could see something happening in 'his' suite.'

'Oh, good plan! Thank you.' I thought a moment, then collected the spare lamp I'd been cleaning as an excuse for going up myself. 'Nick,' I said, emerging from the lift and automatically swerving right in order to avoid the sight of the pele stair door. 'Could I have a word?'

'Sure, what is it?'

Too late, I realised his carpenter was with him, both of them with clipboards and pencils, clearly discussing the alterations. They looked at me enquiringly.

I stopped, disconcerted and frustrated. The need to know what I was missing was urgent and overwhelming, but I didn't really want an audience when I found out. 'Um, can you pop into the office when you've got a moment?' I said lamely. 'I'm just going to store the lamp in the cupola, then I'll be back down there.'

There was a split second where Nick met my eyes. 'We've about finished,' he said evenly. 'I'll come with you.' Another tiny pause. 'Oh, while I remember, there's stuff in this closet that will need clearing out before we start pulling the walls down.'

Closet? I couldn't even think straight right now, the last thing I needed was more delay. But he was gesturing towards the large walk-in cupboard in the far corner, and the carpenter was looking on, so I pulled open the door quickly and we went in. All the rooms in the tower had these storage cupboards. Part wardrobe, part glory-hole, they had a rail for hanging, half a wall of shelves, and enough floor space that you could fit a child's cot inside at a pinch. My ancestors probably squeezed in two. They were perfect for your belongings if you were actually living here, but not so clever as part of a hotel bedroom. By knocking them out, it would free up space for an en-suite.

I knew there would be nothing of mine inside this one because I'd always slept in the main house. Here in the tower I'd have been constantly aware of the pele stair snaking up the inner corner. The very thought of trying to get to sleep with it that close, just waiting for me, made me shudder.

I focussed on the cupboard. The sooner I'd checked it, the sooner I could talk to Nick. The rail held a torn cagoule, there were a couple of ancient sweaters on one of the shelves, a box of cars and books on the floor. 'It looks like left-behind cousin stuff,' I said. 'They used to have a rota for who slept on which floor each holiday. None of it will be wanted. The clothes can go for recycling. Toys and books I'll take to the charity shop, unless there's anything your nephew might like.'

As I turned to go, I spotted a stack of variously coloured ledgers at the back of the highest shelf. They didn't look to have been disturbed for years. Blast. More delay. I gave the lantern to Nick to hold, balanced on a stool and pulled them out, sneezing at the dust. And felt a huge whump of guilt when the note on top read 'Fairlight Accounts' in old-fashioned writing. These were real Fairlights things — and in my haste to talk to Nick, I'd nearly consigned them to the skip! A fragile purple ribbon keeping the bundle together parted company as I lifted it down. For some reason, that made me feel even worse.

'How peculiar,' I said. 'These are to do with Fairlights, but all the family records ought to be in the archive. I wonder if Dad knows about them.' I sneezed again, my arms full of old paper. 'I'll look through them down-stairs after I've put the lantern back.'

Nick was silent. My heart sank. What was the matter now? Was it because I'd mentioned the cousins? I hadn't asked him about my missing memory yet. How was I supposed to do that if he'd turned uncooperative? Oh, why were men so *touchy*?

The lift was still at the top floor. We went in and I pressed the roof button with one elbow.

Nick weighed the lantern in his hands, then looked up. 'You're not claustrophobic, Sorcha,' he said, his voice flat. 'You had no problem with that cupboard and you aren't bothered by the lift. I didn't think you could be when you never acted as if you were before. So why lie? Why pretend you were when we were looking at the pele stair? To make yourself more interesting? To make me feel sorry for you? I don't get it.'

My knees buckled as though he'd pulled a rug from under me. I was astonished to find myself still standing. I was *astoundingly* hurt by his accusation (something that gave me considerable food for thought later). I liked Nick. I'd come straight from the realisation that I'd lost a significant slab of memory to ask him what terrible thing it was that I'd done — and before I could say a word, he had cold-bloodedly set me up to test me on something from several days ago, something that he'd *seen* had bothered the hell out of me. The lift stopped, but I couldn't move. I stared at him, scrabbling for words. 'Before when?' I asked feebly.

'Stop playing games, Sorcha! You know exactly what I'm talking about.'

But I didn't. I really didn't. I didn't know what to say. I didn't know what to do. I forced myself outside on legs that felt as if they belonged to someone else, and paid the price for not concentrating when the wind on the roof of the tower immediately blasted the dust from the books into my eyes and snatched hard at the old fragile pages.

Clutching them to my body, I made a dive for the cupola. Nick flung himself down opposite me. I struggled with the sick feeling in my chest and said, 'Nick, I'm sorry if I'm not making sense this afternoon, but I've had an appalling shock. I don't know how to say this in any way that you'll believe, but I honestly have no idea what you are talking about.'

His face darkened. 'I'm talking about before I left home. I'm talking about you and me.'

There had been a him and me? I was even more panicked. It was what Laurel had implied, but . . . a proper relationship? How could that possibly have happened and me not remember it? 'When?' I asked faintly.

This time he let out a yell of frustration for which I didn't, in retrospect, blame him one bit. 'Fifteen years ago, Sorcha! Fifteen years ago when Ma remarried and I was desperate to get away. You said you'd come with me. You *promised*. And I waited and you didn't show. So I left alone.'

I gaped. There were no words on my lips. There was barely any breath in my lungs.

He was still yelling, on his feet now,

pacing from one end of the cupola to the other and back again. 'Dammit, I knew it was going to be awkward working with you, but I thought at least you'd acknowledge what we'd had back then. I thought you'd make a reference to it. I even thought there was an outside chance I might get some sort of explanation. But you act as if it never happened! I can't *deal* with this, Sorcha.' And with that he slammed back across the roof to the lift and disappeared from view.

I just sat, one hand on the pile of books, one hand to my breast, my eyes on the space where he no longer was. I just sat, listening to the wind swirling in from the sea, chasing around the cupola and racing inland to lose itself in the hills.

I was empty, echoing, and yet with such a roar of questions in my head that I felt nothing any more would ever make any sense. What was happening to me? What was going wrong with my mind? What in Heaven's name had taken place between Nick Marten and me fifteen years ago?

And why did I not remember?

*   *   *

'He didn't even listen to me.'

I had found Annabel and Granny in the kitchen, swapping recipes. I sat down numbly with the old ledgers. I wasn't even sure why I was still cradling them. It was just something for my arms to do.

Granny glanced at me sharply, and cut me a slice of moist, sticky ginger cake. 'Didn't listen to you about what? What have you got there?'

'Thanks.' I took a bite gratefully, the edge of my shock wearing off with the warmth of the treacle and smooth kick of ginger in my mouth. People might decry it, but there is a great deal to be said for cake. I took another bite and lifted the pile of books onto the table. 'These are old Fairlights accounts, according to the note on top. I don't know why they're here instead of in the

County Record Office with everything else.'

'Old is right,' said Annabel. 'Honey, you're covered in cobwebs.'

I opened the top book carefully. The cover was brittle with age, the paper inside surprisingly white. The writing was brown and spiky, as if a packet of dolls' house kindling had been emptied onto the page. I made out the first line with difficulty.

. . . being the daily account of the Fairlight by me, Hannah Ravell . . .

'Oh!' I said in surprise. 'It isn't accounts as in finances, it's accounts as in a diary. And not 'Fairlights', but the Fairlight itself. It's by a Hannah Ravell.'

I read the entry more carefully. This had evidently been written very early on in the history of the house, as Hannah talked of going up and down to the Fairlight via the pele stair. Rather her than me.

'Apparently there was a high wind and the lantern kept going out,' I said to the others as I read. 'But the men were still at sea, so Hannah stayed up on the roof and her husband's sister Mary brought shawls and broth. Gosh, this is ancient. I'm going to have to transcribe it properly.'

'What sort of broth?' asked Annabel. 'What's the year? I could do a themed menu from Fairlights history when we open.'

I looked back at the beginning. 'It doesn't say. I can work it out from the main records by searching for when a Hannah and a Mary were both alive. As for the broth, they'd have used whatever they had, I suppose. They'd have kept chickens, wouldn't they, Granny? I imagine there was always fish. Nothing would have gone to waste.'

'Where did you find these?' asked Granny, touching the books with a wondering look. 'My mother-in-law sometimes talked about 'the accounts', but she never showed them to me.'

'How mean,' said Annabel.

Granny shrugged. 'She was a difficult woman; she enjoyed martyring herself

99

on the roof with the light and liked being the sole responsible one. She drank up the praise and swelled with the importance of doing her duty by Fairlights, and was outraged when Trinity House said the Fairlight was no longer necessary for modern shipping. I think it turned her mind a little. She vowed to keep it going as a private light. Thought of herself as the last custodian, and expected people to run around after her because of it.'

'Charming,' said Annabel.

'As I say, odd. I believe she'd have been completely untroubled living in a proper lighthouse on a rock in the middle of the Atlantic.' Granny made a rueful face. 'I often wished she was. She was very scornful about my fear of heights. She said there was no point showing me how to set things up, I could just make myself useful cleaning the lamps and polishing the lenses for her down here. And she was furious with me for only bearing sons, not daughters for her to mould in her image. That was the one thing I was glad of at the time. I wouldn't have put it past her to snatch any baby girl away from me at birth and wall herself up with her in the pele.'

'Granny, how horrible! She sounds completely dotty. I don't expect it helped that you cooked better than her either.'

'I wouldn't know. She never lifted a finger in the kitchen after I married John. You'll have gathered I wasn't the suitably cowed bride she'd chosen for him.'

Annabel made a rude noise. I grinned. 'Well, I'm glad he found you for himself then. These diaries, or whatever they are, were in the walk-in cupboard on the top floor of the pele. Right at the back of the high shelf.'

'That makes sense. That was Phyllis's room when John first brought me here,' said Granny. 'Close to the Fairlight, see? She'll have kept them there on purpose, even after she moved lower. The only time I ever went that high was to change the bedding. I don't mind the view from down here, because I can't see the drop to the beach. I can't take it in the tower.'

Hannah Ravell's writing required too much concentration. I gave up and leafed gently through the pages. 'Oh!' I said suddenly. The handwriting had changed. 'Oh, I see! They *all* wrote in it. That's why the handwriting changes and why there are so many journals. All the women who took over the Fairlight took over the daily accounts too. My word, Dad is going to *adore* these. I'll ring him later to tell him.'

It was rather lovely, all these different Ravells, linked by duty throughout the centuries. I'd often wondered why there were no entries by the women of the house in the Fairlights family papers. They must have used these diary pages instead. I spotted a round, easy-to-read script. This writer was much chattier than Hannah.

. . . Westerly gales yesterday, just now dying down. The fishing is always

good in a westerly, but at such cost!
Anne Trent has lost her husband and
both eldest boys and will need suc-
cour this winter. The new wing remains
sound in the wind, thank the Lord. I
hope our guests are not too distressed
by this weather. I was near blown off
the tower last night. Fortunately the
fairwives lent me their strength. When
my dear Robin's mama first told me
of them, I did not understand her,
but I have now been several times
very glad of their aid . . .

I looked up. 'Who were the fairwives?
There's a mention of them helping with
the light.'

Granny shook her head. 'I don't
know. John's mother kept everything
to herself. I thought it was only ever
the family who looked after the light.
Although that said, the couple of times
it's been needed when I've been alone
here, one of the lifeboat men has come
up from the village to see to it. Phyllis
used to say 'Men fish, women get them

home'.' She faltered. 'Mostly.'

Annabel and I exchanged a swift glance. In an instant, my friend was proposing a clafoutis for tonight's dessert and wondering what soft fruit Granny might have available for her to use. In the ensuing flurry of activity, the terrible storm during which my grandfather's boat was lost, was pushed to the back of her mind.

I went back to the entry.

. . . the shelter is in splinters after the gale. Robin is to build a hexagonal one as being a sturdier shape. He has been drawing it all morning, asking me what I think. He is full of plans and I fear it will be a much grander affair than necessary, but he does love these projects, and I love him, so will admire and marvel — and hope to introduce a little practicality where I can.

Reading those words, my eyes prickled. I didn't even know her name, yet this candid, cheerful ancestor of mine had touched my heart. I did hope our current cupola was the same one her Robin had designed.

I leafed back, discovered she was Charlotte Ravell and had taken over the account in 1812. I finished my tea and shut the journal. I would read more later. Outside, Nick Marten strode past the window on his way home. I felt a jolt to my shoulders as the real world intervened.

'So,' I said aloud, 'do either of you have any idea how I can convince Nick I've lost part of my memory?'

Granny emerged from the larder, a bowl of cherries in her hand. 'Oh no, dear. Not again? How did it happen this time?'

Shock ripped through me. It was the last thing I'd expected her to say. '*Again?* What do you mean — again?'

'It happened before, darling. Years ago, when you fell down the pele stair.'

I stared at her, my hand automatically going out to clutch Annabel's. 'When I did what?'

'Fell down the pele stair. Surely you've been told by now? The rest of us had been out for the day — an agricultural show, I think, I can't remember now — and when we got back, there you were, white as bleached driftwood, asleep at the bottom of the pele stair. You'd fallen and hit your head. The doctor said you must have been unconscious for a while before you slept. You'd lost quite a bit of blood. Oh, Sorcha, my heart turned over when I saw you there. Your poor arms and legs were cut and bruised and your fingertips were all bloodied. Your mother started scream- ing and your father ran straight to the phone for an ambulance. It was a good thing the boys had stuffed themselves at the food tent. No one got anything to eat until about midnight.'

I couldn't speak. I was stunned. I didn't remember this at all.

Granny was continuing. 'Of course, we got you to hospital right away. The ambulance was quick, I'll give them that. We sent the boys along the road to watch for it and direct it in. Tristram thought they were out looking for him! He was most put out to have missed the drama. His own fault for insisting on driving himself in his own car, not travelling with the rest of us. Funny, isn't it? At one time you couldn't get him out of his car. Now you can't get him into one.'

'He drives in London, but for long journeys he prefers the train so he can work on it,' I said distractedly. 'Tell me more about *me*. I don't know this at all.'

'Nothing to be told. We never did find out what had happened. Your parents took you straight home from the hospital. It was a sad ending to the holiday. You'd been so very happy that summer, all alive and glowing. It made me smile just to look at you. Your mother said you never referred to the accident after you got home, and no one liked to ask what had happened in case it disrupted your recovery.'

Evidently I hadn't mentioned it,

because the bang on the head had made me lose my memory! I'd heard of cases like that, but had never met anyone it had actually happened to. I was struggling to take it in. However, it did solve why I'd always had such an uneasy feeling about the pele stair. I was very relieved to have *that* explained.

Granny returned to the larder. 'What really puzzled us,' she said, fetching enough potatoes for an army out of the vegetable rack, 'was why you were on the pele stair in the first place.'

My relief drained abruptly away. A tiny prickle of cold settled on my spine. 'What do you mean?'

'You'd always been so terrified of it. Right from when you were a little girl and got shut in there. My goodness the noise you made! I can hear you now. You rushed out yelling your head off, screaming and shouting about darkness and fire. It took hours to calm you down. Nothing would ever get you past the door after that. You refused even to look through the open doorway from a distance to prove there was nothing there.'

The cold feeling in my spine intensified. So the accident *hadn't* been why I was afraid of the pele stair after all. But darkness and fire? I swallowed. That was impossible. I'd only recently had a precognition about darkness and fire in the pele, down by the jetty on my first evening back. How could it have already happened?

*　*　*

We were sitting down to dinner when Annabel's mobile bleeped with a text summoning her in to work the following day due to staff sickness. After a grumble about her break being cut short and certain people being first against the wall when she ruled the world, she addressed herself to her phone and worked out that if I could get her to Carlisle station for the early train, she could just about make her shift.

That gave us an excuse not to stay up

late, for which I was very grateful. I still needed to come to terms with the shocks of the day in private. On top of that, Tristram was being a pain, restless and jumpy and *tremendously* amusing about the provincial nature of the workforce, saying we girls would need regular away-days to London if we ever got the hotel off the ground, in order to get some decent conversation and feed our killer heel habit. I swear I have never come so close to thumping him.

In contrast, Alastair's enthusiasm over a specialist sea-angling equipment website was almost soothing. Which, as I said to Annabel as we scooped Granny up with us and bore her off to bed, leaving the men to fend for themselves, was something I never thought I'd hear myself say.

'Life's full of surprises,' said Annabel.

Maybe so, but I'd quite like them to stop now. I'd had as many surprises as I could take today.

6

I slept appallingly. Quite apart from the overload of revelations I'd had recently, I kept waking with sections of the Fairlights accounts in my head, and other entries that I didn't think I'd read, but seemed somehow to fit. So many of my jumbled, fragmented dreams turned into running up the pele stair — both as I'd remembered it for years and as I'd seen it with Nick — that they drove me out of bed towards dawn to make tea and try to regain some perspective on the world.

There was a light on in the kitchen. Granny was sitting at the table reading the most recent of the journals. She looked more deeply unhappy than I had ever seen her.

'Granny?' I said, hurrying across the stone-flagged floor. 'Darling, you're frozen. Are you all right? What are you doing down here?' Her tea was untouched, the pot cold in front of her.

'The entries stop in 1966,' she said in a lost voice. 'That was when Phyllis had her stroke. She never walked or talked again.'

I had a moment of appalled realisation. How *selfish* of me. I had been thinking of the accounts as historical, written by my long-ago ancestors. But of course the entries had continued down through the years. And naturally someone as obsessed with the Fairlight as my great-grandmother would have relished the opportunity to add her contribution to the journals. She'd probably snatched the pen from her mother-in-law's fingers. Making her mark. The last custodian.

'Oh, Granny,' I said, mortified. 'I hadn't even thought she'd have written in it too. Are you okay?'

Granny made a small, forlorn movement. 'I already knew she disliked me. At least now I know it wasn't just me. She was equally disappointed with John's father for not giving her any more children, and with John for thwarting her plans and marrying me. She really detested Trinity House. There are holes in some of these pages where she'd pressed so hard with her pen that she'd gone through. I wonder . . . ' She broke off. 'I do wonder if there wasn't just a touch of insanity there.'

'It certainly sounds like it,' I said cheerfully. 'But I'm pretty sure it hasn't come through to me, so we're okay.'

But Granny wasn't finished yet. I could tell there was more she needed to get off her chest. I put the kettle on again and said, 'She sounds thoroughly unpleasant. What happened after she had her stroke?'

'Nothing. I fed her, cleaned her, we had the District Nurse in once a day. She'd already shifted down to the first floor of the pele, so we looked after her there. John did suggest it might be easier for the nursing if she was in the farmhouse — but she had a way of sucking all the happiness out of you and neither of us wanted her that close to us or the boys. She was like that for over a year. And then 1967 brought dreadful autumn storms. Mostly the men stayed ashore during them, but this one blew up out of nowhere. It was awful, Sorcha. All the power was out. Rain beating at the windows. John had been out on the boat since dawn and I had three small boys to care for. I fed Phyllis mouthfuls of soup and she spat it back. I could feel her hatred burning into me for being so feeble. Burning me for my cowardice. It was horrible.'

Granny's voice cracked, telling me what had been so long buried. I rubbed her hand comfortingly, but she didn't want to be comforted.

'I tried going up the tower to set the Fairlight, I really did, even though no one had ever shown me what to do. The lift was out, but I could manage the flights of stairs if I kept my eyes straight ahead. But oh, Sorcha, once I was on the roof . . . It was terrifying. The whole world swooped and did nosedives around me. And it was so wet and so cold. I crawled across, hardly able to

114

move. I heard voices on the wind. I thought I was going mad, I really did.'

'Oh, Granny.'

Now she did take my hand. 'I made it up the first step to the cupola, but it took so long and I was dizzy and retching. I thought, if I died up here, who would look after the boys? I know I was weeping. Then the oddest thing — I felt an arm around my shoulders, and hands helping me back to the stairs. There was a gentle voice in my ear telling me to return to my children. I knew it was my imagination, my subconscious playing an extreme trick to get me back to my babies, but it seemed real and I was so grateful. I'd got frozen, you see, frozen mentally as well as frozen physically. I wouldn't have been able to move without that voice, not unless I'd heard one of the boys crying. And I couldn't have heard anything up there.'

I squeezed her hand.

She went on, dry eyed. 'They found parts of John's boat the next day, miles and miles down the coast. They never found the men.' Granny paused. 'And I know it might have happened even before I set foot on the staircase, and I know it might not have made any difference even if I'd got the Fairlight going, but it doesn't help.'

'You survived the night though, Granny. You survived to look after Dad and Uncle Michael and Uncle Anthony. It could have been so much worse.' I let her go so I could make the tea.

Granny sighed. 'I suppose so. And then,' she added in a stronger voice, 'do you know what that evil woman did? She died a week later! I swear it was on purpose, just so she could get in the way of my arrangements for John and add even more guilt to my grief.'

I hugged her without words, just as she used to comfort me as a child when the cousins were teasing me. I wondered if she'd ever told anyone the full story of that awful night before. I reached across her to close the journal on the black, unforgiving writing of her mother-in-law. 'It's over,' I said. 'From everything you've ever told me about Grandad, he wouldn't have wanted you to have done things any differently.'

'Bless you, love, I know it, but sometimes when the wind comes and the rain lashes, I can feel her hatred stalking me even after all this time. I'll take my tea to bed for a little while, I think. It's brought it all back. You'll be all right down here?'

'I'll be fine.'

Still she lingered, the steam rising from her mug. 'It's why I can't ever leave, Sorcha. I know the family means well, but John will know to find me here.'

I had doubts that Tristram had meant particularly well when he was pressuring her into selling Fairlights and buying a nice modern bungalow on a new estate in town, but I said, 'You don't have to leave Fairlights ever, Granny. I'm here now, and I'm staying.'

Granny cast a last look at the journals. 'Stupid of me. I just had to know what she'd said.'

'I know.'

After she'd gone, my hand hovered over the book. No, I decided, putting it at the end of the stack. I would look at Phyllis's journal entries when I came to them in the proper sequence. Not now.

I could have taken the journals back to bed myself, but it seemed somehow right to read the entries in this farmhouse kitchen where so many of them must have been written. I went back to Charlotte Ravell's section. What Granny had said about voices urging her on, a warm arm laid across her shoulders, reminded me of something Charlotte had mentioned about 'the fairwives' lending her their aid. Looking for the entry, I was distracted by finding what must have been the original plans for the cupola tucked between the pages. I was ridiculously pleased to realise that her husband's hexagonal design really *was* the one still in place today. Better still, Robin had sketched a tiny figure in the corner, an impish blonde woman in a long blue hooded cloak setting a lantern on a dais. It had to be Charlotte. I felt a daft warm flutter of recognition and touched her gently before putting the plan carefully aside to show Nick. I knew he'd be interested.

Which brought me back with a crash to my missing memories. And Nick Marten himself. Come hell or high water, I wasn't going to let another day pass with this still unresolved. I'd take Annabel to the station, give Mum a ring to find out what had happened after they'd discovered me, then I'd search him out. He could be as unfriendly as he pleased, but I had to tell him I hadn't stood him up deliberately all those years ago.

* * *

'Where did you go when you left home?' I asked.

Nick looked up warily from his desk. I'd fetched us two mugs of proper coffee and several slices of the ginger cake which I put in the space between us. I hoped he'd see it as a peace offering.

Apparently he did. Either that or he was holding fire for the time being. He nodded for me to sit down. 'I followed my father to Edinburgh. He wasn't overjoyed to see me, but he did his duty by me and fixed me up with an apprenticeship in the industry and day release at the local college.'

I took a deep breath. 'I wasn't lying, Nick. I really don't remember a single thing. Granny told me yesterday afternoon that they came back from a day out towards the end of one summer and found me unconscious at the base of the pele stair. I'm guessing that was the day you were talking about.'

He half rose in alarm. 'Unconscious?'

'I'd fallen, hit my head, lost some blood. Nobody knew how long I'd been there. I was covered in cuts and bruises apparently. They rushed me to hospital where I was kept in for a while, and

120

then I went straight home to London from there. I phoned Mum up this morning to see what the doctors had said. They ran a battery of tests, but the consensus was that there was no lasting damage apart from the memory loss, and that I'd been very lucky. The thing is, Nick, I don't remember any of that summer at all. More to the point, I didn't even realise that I'd forgotten it.'

'How could you not know?'

I took a sip of my coffee. Nick's eyes were still on me. Tense as I was, I had to admit to a tiny flicker of gratification that he was alarmed about my accident, even fifteen years on.

A knock at the door was followed by the carpenter, mouth open to ask a question. He looked from Nick to me and said he'd pop back later.

The interruption had eased the tension. I met Nick's eyes frankly. 'How could I not know I'd lost a whole summer? It's a fair question. I'm not sure I can explain it properly, but I'll give it a try. It's historical, really. Whenever I've been at Fairlights — especially when I was younger — it's always as if it has been separate from real time. We'd come every holiday, pick up village life here as if we'd never been away, go home for the beginning of a new term, pick up school life again. No overlap. So when I woke up at home at the beginning of the Autumn term with a fading set of bruises down one side and a slightly fuzzy head, I was so used to slipping back into the London routine that all my energy went into the new term and getting to grips with our GCSE year. Yesterday, after Granny told me, I sat down with Annabel and tried to recall all the separate summers here. I remember the time I was fourteen when you won the stone-skimming championship — we didn't have anything going on then together, did we?'

Nick shook his head.

'And I remember Christmas that year, when Dad and Finn and I had to light the Fairlight and then we sat up in the cupola chatting about duty and history and how it didn't matter what we did in life as long as we loved it, did it to the best of our ability, and it didn't hurt anyone. And if we *did* have to sponge on anyone, then at least we should give value for money in return. Looking back on it, I think that was probably directed at Finn rather than me, but I took it as a licence later on not to bother with university, but to get a job as an office girl in the local hotel and do Business Studies in the evenings instead. Anyway, I don't recall being at Fairlights aged fifteen at all. Not at all. Christmas, maybe, because I spent it wrapped in a duvet in my bedroom revising for Mocks. The next summer in my memory is when I was sixteen. Annabel came with me for the first time. GCSEs were over, so we had an extra month up here. She was going through a bad patch. It rained. We spent most of the holiday talking about ourselves, cleaning lamps, cooking and listening to music. I don't remember you being in the village.'

'I wasn't,' said Nick. 'I was learning the trade on a country house restoration in Derbyshire. It was a terrific placement, but I did miss the sea. I would have come back for a weekend, except Laurel wrote and told me you were at Fairlights.'

'I don't remember Laurel either, and I didn't know you had a step-father.'

'Ma and Clive had married just after Easter, so that was Laurel's first summer with us. She was a skinny, undersized twelve-year-old and her father was a bully. She hero-worshipped me because I stood up to him. It didn't last. I couldn't bear him, and the arguments were making Ma unhappy and him worse. So I left, and let them both down.'

'Probably the best thing you could have done. Laurel really hates me, by the way. I'm so sorry, Nick. I wish I could tell you what happened, but I don't know. I don't even know why I was on the pele stair. I realise it's not claustrophobia now, but I've always been terrified of the bloody thing. Granny said I got stuck in there when I was tiny and came out screaming about darkness and fire. They said I was claustrophobic — so I assumed I was because of being told it so often. I never even thought about not getting panicky in other small confined spaces.'

Silence settled on us. Steam curled up from our coffee mugs and twined together. Nick reached through it for my hand. 'I'm sorry too. And I'm sorry I blew up at you yesterday without listening to you. All these years I've thought . . . ' He broke off, shaking his head. 'It's not important now. Just like that, it's not important. It's surprisingly liberating, letting go. I hadn't realised. Just tell me, Sorcha. This thing — us, even if you don't remember it — is it still there for you?'

The knowledge I'd felt before swept through me, or maybe it was new knowledge, born of our grown-up selves. 'Oh, yes,' I said simply.

His hand tightened. I think we might have tried a first awkward kiss, but we heard voices on the veranda and Tristram and Alastair came past the window.

Nick's lips thinned. 'At least that's one thing to be grateful for. You didn't get together with your dear cousin Tristram either.'

'Tris?' I yelped. 'Good God, no. Why ever would I?'

Nick pulled some plans across the desk to make it look as though we were studying them. 'Because . . . '

Too late. I didn't have any time to do more than peer intelligently at Nick's pointing finger before Alastair and my cousin were upon us.

'We've decided to change the time-table and convert the tower first,' said Tristram. 'The sooner we can get paying customers through the door the better for the finances.'

Non-functioning in other areas I might be, but I wasn't going to let this pass without a fight. I sat back and folded my arms. 'Oh yes, it is going to look just *so* professional having luxury en-suite bedrooms with a price tag to match and then asking guests to picnic off sandwiches at one end of the restaurant. Not to mention stepping over dust sheets as they come through Reception and moving carpenters' trestles out of the way in order to get a drink at the bar. Just how did you make all your money, Tris?'

His expression darkened at the criticism. 'Your timescale won't have us turning a profit for six months.'

'Yours won't have us turning a profit at all. I gave you my forward plan and you agreed it. This is *my business*, Tristram. I do wish you'd trust me not to cut my own throat.'

Alastair interrupted. 'But, Sorcha, there's a house-breaking sale thirty miles away. They've got period furniture dirt cheap and the most perfect Edwardian staircase. It would match the tower lift beautifully.'

'So buy it,' said Nick lazily. 'The standard staircase is due for refurbishment anyway. Easier to store the new one in place rather than in the barns. Just draw my lads the plans.'

'I suppose,' I said, looking at him enquiringly, 'we could start converting, say, the top floor of the pele as a show apartment for the brochure? We can still keep the Regency wing downstairs on schedule and it would only put back the upstairs a little bit.'

Alastair tried to look cool at the suggestion, but excitement threatened to break out all over him.

'I'll look into it,' replied Nick, straight-faced.

Tristram seemed grudgingly appeased. I moved to the doorway and watched them go towards Alastair's office. 'Any bets on whether we get shot of them before we turn that room into the bar? They only want to change the schedule because Alastair fancies moving into the tower and going sea-angling on your brother-in-law's boat at every opportunity. He probably thinks he's going to get the top apartment at a discount because of being Tristram's pal.'

'And won't he?'

I gave him a swift smile. 'Not a chance. The hotel is my concern, my livelihood. Tris is lending us the money in return for a stake in the profits. You've heard him on the phone to other people, he'll want repaying. I could have financed the conversion through the bank, but it's better keeping the money in the family. It's also faster, with fewer conditions, and most important of all, it means Granny can stay on here without a break, now she's got me to keep an eye on her full time.'

Nick leaned back in his chair. 'Let me get this straight. Your cousin can fund a speculative venture, but not pay for a carer for his grandmother in order for her to stay in her own house?'

'That's Tristram. Nick, do you believe me about losing my memory?'

He made a helpless gesture. 'I have to. It's the only thing that makes sense. It must have been one hell of a crack on the head.'

I felt a great rush of relief. 'According

to my mother, it really was. The specialist said I might never get that memory back, and warned her not to even try pushing me for it. She threatened the rest of the family with everlasting hellfire if anyone so much as whispered about it — so that's why it was never mentioned. And then most people forgot anyway.'

'You could have been killed.'

'Yes.' I was silent. 'It's a bit sobering, isn't it? But I wasn't. Nick, when can we talk properly?'

But even as he drew breath, my mobile rang and his email beeped. Tris's voice carried loudly down from Alastair's office.

'Not here, not now,' Nick murmured. 'After work. We'll go for a stroll along the beach.'

'It's a date,' I replied, and answered my phone.

7

The phone call was from Erin.

'I've tried everybody else,' she started off without preamble. 'So now I'm ringing you. Do *not* tell me Tristram isn't up to something. You don't live with a man for fourteen years and not know when his mind is elsewhere. What's going on? For a start, where's that bosomy friend of yours?'

'Hello, Erin,' I said pleasantly. 'I have no idea what has got into Tris, but I wish it hadn't. He's being an absolute pain. He's interfering with the building work right, left and centre.'

'Because he knows what he's doing,' she snapped. 'You should listen to him, Sorcha. He's made a lot more money than you by being right.'

This was actually quite encouraging. Erin was mad as fire, but still leaping instantly into Tristram-support mode at the first sign of criticism. Nothing could be irretrievably wrong from her perspective if she was still presenting a united front.

'Whatever's the matter with him, it isn't Annabel,' I said. 'She was only here a couple of days and was with me or Granny all the time. There was no evidence of any interest between them at all.'

'Where is she now?'

'Back at work, of course. And if I take my phone out into the lobby, you'll be able to hear Tris talking at the top of his voice to Alastair. I tell you, the pair of them are driving me demented.'

There was a grudging silence. Then, 'So which other women are up there?'

I lost patience with her. 'None! For goodness sake, Erin, if you think Tris is playing away, park the kids with your parents and book yourselves a dirty weekend in Paris. That should do it.'

'Huh,' she said, a sour note in her voice. 'What makes you think he'd want to come?'

'Oh, let me see, aside from the fact that you have the best figure of any woman I know? Make it an expensive dirty weekend — and use his credit card. The day my cousin doesn't extract maximum value out of his own money is the day you really need to worry about him.'

She brooded for a moment. 'It's definitely not Annabel?'

'Definitely not Annabel.'

'Well then,' she said, 'if I'm using his card, I might as well make it a week. Where's good this time of year?'

A while later, there was a roar of fury from the other side of the Regency wing. I kept my head down, working on the new schedule. Sure enough, my cousin strode through the door, simmering with irritation. 'I'm off,' he said. 'Erin's run mad. She's booked us a bloody week in the Caribbean, leaving this Friday. Said it was a bargain.'

'That's nice,' I said.

He glared at me. 'What she doesn't grasp is that the money for her bargains comes from my investments which I have to keep up to the mark — and I can't if I'm on the far side of the world!'

'Just as well we don't need our hands holding here, then, isn't it?'

'So you say.'

I ignored the rudeness. 'So I know. The team is doing really well.'

He eyed me balefully. 'We should have gone with Alastair's boys. It would have been finished in half the time.'

'Don't start this again, Tris. The change of use for Fairlights depended on us using local labour, and even if it hadn't, I need village goodwill to run the hotel efficiently. You're not picking a fight with me, cousin dear. I won't rise. Take your bad temper out on British Rail on your way home.'

Still Tristram stood there, glowering. Through the window to the courtyard, I heard the sound of a van arriving with a delivery. The smell of newly sawn wood drifted through the building on an autumnal sea breeze. Next door, Nick was on the phone to one of our suppliers, businesslike and friendly. It occurred to me that the butler in the old days must have sat right where I was, leisurely polishing his silver, a light hand on the threads of his household. Certainly he'd have been listening (like I was to Nick) for any altercations in the card room, ready to move in a stately fashion to defuse them. My gaze fell on my fingers where I could still feel Nick's brief hand clasp. My pulse rate increased a notch. 'Go, Tris,' I said. 'I'm busy. We're all busy. It's only a week's holiday. You might even enjoy it.'

He looked at my desk, covered in multi-coloured lists, and made a jerky movement. 'Is this really what you want, Sorcha? To be stuck up here with these yokels? You haven't even got a view.'

I met his eyes in astonishment. 'Are you serious? Of course it's what I want! This is my office, my empire. It's my dream come true! Why would I have sunk everything I own in Fairlights

135

otherwise? My own hotel, working with grand people, in the place I love best in all the world. Just let me get *on* with it.'

★   ★   ★

I thought I'd been frantic to hear what Nick had to tell me about my lost summer, but now I knew he *could*, it took second place to the butterfly-excitement of there no longer being a shadow between us.

By unspoken consent we both worked until everyone had finished for the day, and then went down to the beach via the cliff steps (which, despite what Nick had said, were *nothing* like the pele tower stair). It was quiet at the bottom of the cliff, the surface of the sand was crisp and untouched. Like my heart, I thought, treasuring the pulse-racing moment before Nick stepped down beside me and took me into his arms.

I wish I could say my memory returned at the first touch of his lips, but it didn't. What I did feel was completely, utterly safe. To use a well-worn cliché, it felt like coming home.

'All these years, I thought I'd put you out of my mind,' murmured Nick, threading his hands in my hair. 'But you were there all along.' He bent his mouth to mine again.

Eventually we came enough to our senses to start walking. 'I hate not knowing about us,' I said. 'How long were we together that summer?'

'Almost all of it,' replied Nick. 'You came across me at the jetty early on, having a shouting match with my step-father. When he broke it off and strode away, you offered me the use of the Fairlights rowing boat to get it out of my system. We already knew each other, of course, as part of the crowd, so it was probably just a friendly gesture on your part. But then you hopped in opposite me, fearless as anything. Considering my state of mind at the time, I thought that was pretty damn impressive. You sat there as I rowed hard out of the harbour, listening to me ranting about the unfairness of life. And once I was calmer, you guided us back in with the Fairlight rhyme and the leading marks. I think it was the most faith anyone has shown in me ever. We spent the rest of the day together, just walking and talking, until it was time for both of us to get back to our respective homes for tea.'

And I couldn't recall any of it. Not a thing. It was like a growling pain under my present happiness. 'Where is he now, your step-father?'

'Long gone. Went out to work on the oil rigs, never came back. Ma's better off without him.'

'Why don't you and Tristram get on?'

Nick gave a humourless laugh. 'Him being a supercilious prat isn't enough? There's a bit of history with my sister.'

'Laurel?' I asked, surprised. I would have thought she was too young.

'No, Kathryn. While she was still going out with Donal, your cousin tried to tempt her away with his tall, blond and handsome, lord-of-the-manor act. I didn't like it and said so — I was a very bolshy teenager — and fortunately she saw through him before any damage was done, but he's had a down on both of us ever since.'

I winced. That did sound very Tris, wanting something just because he could. He wouldn't have kept up the relationship after he'd made Kathryn fall in love with him. He'd have been on to the next challenge. 'I apologise,' I said.

'Not your fault. But when you and I started getting interested in each other, he didn't like it one bit. I don't think he'd realised you were growing up until then. All of a sudden, I was a threat in my own right. He never stopped having snide goes at me. Looking back now, I suppose it was fairly comical. He was quite a bit older, you were the only girl cousin and you were escaping from his control. The alpha-male wanting domination over his pack. He's a bit like that still, isn't he?'

'He's a *lot* like that,' I said with

feeling. Nick and I were holding hands as we strolled along the beach. It felt natural, as if we'd walked like this hundreds of times, which of course we had. I was so angry at losing those memories. 'That makes sense, actually,' I said, referring to my cousin's bad behaviour. 'Annabel thought it was me Tristram fancied, even when he was making a pass at her the first year she was here. I still can't see it. The 'wanting to be in control' idea is better. When Annabel was here we were sixteen, joined at the hip, and so self-obsessed it wasn't true. Annabel's parents had just split up, so she was intensely emotional, and being a loyal friend I was with her all the way. At that age, all you want to do is talk things through over and over again. We had our heads together the whole summer — when we weren't talking, we were cooking. Tristram hated that. He made several attempts to break in, then gave up and went hell for leather for Erin, just to show us.'

'Whose daddy happened to be a successful banker, I understand.'

'Yes, but to be fair, I don't think he knew that to start with, though I daresay he found out pretty fast. Erin was seventeen, bored to tears at being carted up here away from her friends, busting out all over ... it was inevitable. Tristram always *has* landed on his feet.'

Nick nodded thoughtfully. 'But the previous year — our year — *he* was the bored one. Kathryn and her friends were all married by then. The other local girls were too young. He saw us becoming closer and couldn't hack it. He made it plain I wasn't welcome at Fairlights. With the hassle I was getting at home, I was in no mood to be placating. So we went for long walks like we're doing now, we kissed on the beach, hung around with the crowd at the harbour. We were intense and innocent and in love.'

My hand clenched on his. 'I hate not remembering! First love only happens once. That accident has robbed me of mine.'

Nick raised my hand to his lips and brought me around to face him. 'We can make new memories, Sorcha. If you want to? I know it's early days still, but . . . '

'I do,' I said. And yes, it did feel like a declaration.

When we reached the end of the beach, we scrambled up onto the quay. Nick reached down an arm to help me. Just the gesture, the our wrists interlocking, made me feel a little gooey inside. I must have got it bad.

A sea fog cloaked the bay, not as thick as it had been on my first night home but solid enough to be disconcerting to a casual visitor. I had a moment's doubt. Would the hotel visitors love this place as much as I did? Windows around the harbour glowed yellow through the mist. On the far side, Grace Ravell's statue rose out of it, all-seeing, all-wise. I remembered I hadn't told Nick about the Fairlights diaries, but ahead of us I saw the tea rooms, just shutting up for the day and I thought of something else.

'Laurel is going to be furious. She hates me so much.'

Nick drew in his breath. 'Ah. That's my fault. She blames you for breaking my heart and causing me to run away, abandoning her. She was only twelve, remember.'

I frowned. 'But you were leaving home in any case. Why would she think it was because of me and not her father?'

He looked slightly discomfited. 'When I reached Edinburgh, I rang to let Ma know where I was. She started wailing and dropped the phone. Laurel picked it up. I was exhausted from the journey, guilty as hell hearing Ma sobbing in the background, sore from the lack of enthusiasm Dad had shown when I arrived on his doorstep, and still raw that you hadn't come with me. I just snapped that I was there safe, alone, and would everyone now please get off my case. Laurel shouted back that she knew I was alone, because she'd seen you go into Fairlights with your cousin Tristram. That just about ripped me in two.'

I turned an appalled face on him. 'When? That day? With *Tristram*? If I did, it would only have been to put him off the scent. How would she have known?'

'I didn't realise at the time, but she'd been spying on us. Jealous, because she'd cast me as her hero, but I was spending all my time with you. That day, she'd hidden behind the gatepost and peered around. She was so skinny you wouldn't have seen her.'

'But Tris has never mentioned any such thing! He was out with the others.'

'All day?'

I made a frustrated movement. 'How would I know? I lost my memory, remember? No, wait . . . ' I shut my eyes, recalling Granny's words. 'He was in his own car that day. Granny said so.' I moved uneasily. 'Did I have a bag, do you know? Did the conversation look friendly?'

Nick glanced across the road to where the tea shop light had just gone out. 'Laurel,' he called.

His step-sister turned her head and walked towards us, her steps slowing and her smile fading as she saw me.

'Hi,' I said awkwardly.

She ignored me. 'I've got to get back,' she said to Nick. 'Jamie needs his tea.'

'Ma will already have done it,' said Nick. 'Tell Sorcha what you saw the day I left. Make it the truth, Laurel.'

Laurel looked at me with unfriendly eyes. 'It was you and your cousin arguing. I couldn't hear at first, then the wind shifted and he said, 'I knew you'd stayed home for a reason. If you're brave enough to run away with that lout, you're brave enough to go up to the top of the pele stair and back.' Then you said that was ridiculous and he said it was either that or you give up the idea altogether. And that you'd be better off with him and he'd make sure you realised it.'

I gasped. 'Tristram said that?'

'I said so, didn't I? Anyway, you picked up your bag and went inside with him.' She looked at Nick. 'Can I go now? I have been working all day, you know.'

'You didn't tell me all that before,' said Nick.

Laurel shrugged. 'Didn't I? Perhaps you didn't ask.'

'And you forgot to tell me Sorcha had a bag.'

She twisted away from him angrily and stalked off. 'What difference does it make!'

'I had a bag,' I repeated softly. 'I'd packed. I'd made an excuse to the family. I *was* coming to meet you, Nick. I was. I knew I couldn't have hurt you deliberately.'

'Even though you don't remember that summer?'

But his eyes were looking less shadowed, the strain lines around the corners had smoothed out. I took his hand and laid it against my heart. 'I know how I feel now,' I said, 'and I don't believe I could have felt any different then.'

'Sorcha . . . '

I shook my head slowly, trying to make sense of it. 'But I still don't understand. Tristram would have known about my phobia over the pele stair. I was terrified of it. Still am. Everyone knows that.'

Which meant he'd made an impossible task the condition of my leaving that day. The control-freak strikes again.

But . . .

But . . .

But if I hadn't managed to talk him out of it, if I'd loved Nick enough to take up the dare (and I could see how I might, even though the thought of it gave me palpitations), then surely my cousin would have heard me scream, he would have known I'd fallen . . .

And he hadn't done anything about it.

Horror crept along my veins. Maybe Tris had panicked and driven off, pretending he'd thought I was all right. I could see him doing that. But there was my bag too. Neither Granny nor Mum had mentioned it. He must have put it back in my room. Unpacked it, even. How could he have just left me? How?

I looked up to see my sickening conclusions mirrored in Nick's face. He gripped my hands and met my eyes sombrely. 'It isn't good, is it. Whichever way you view it. You have to ask Tristram what happened, Sorcha. You can't let this one lie. There isn't a carpet big enough to brush it under. I'll come with you.'

'We can't ask him today. He left this afternoon. He'll be on the train home.'

Nick rubbed his nose. 'Can't say I'm sorry.'

A shaky grin tugged at my mouth. 'Nor me.'

He put his arm around my waist and we walked to the jetty, our footsteps deadened by the fog. Grace Ravell stood before us, her flaming torch raised, her eyes scanning the horizon in calm certainty that all she needed was resolution. I stood on the plinth and reached up to curl my left hand around hers. The carved wood was smooth and reassuring. All would be well. Nick put his hands around my waist to lift me down and this time there was no precognition to tell me what I already knew would happen. 'So where do you touch her?' I asked him, laughing.

For answer, he reached up and cradled her waist, just as he'd done with me. I felt an absurd happiness as I kissed him properly and the mist circled gently around us.

★　★　★

I invited Nick back for supper, making the 19th century drawing of the cupola that I'd found in the Fairlight accounts the excuse. Not that I needed an excuse for Granny, but I suspected Tristram would be in touch with Alastair and I didn't want any gossip seeping through the family, courtesy of Erin. This was very new, still. We wanted to keep it precious and private and all to ourselves for the moment.

Nick and Alastair were both delighted with Robin Ravell's detailed original plans. They plunged into the sort of technical conversation that meant they might as well have been talking a different language as far as Granny and I were concerned. After the meal, Alastair bore the drawing away to make a copy, but Nick stayed, leafing through the Fairlights diary entries as he sipped his coffee. I sat next to him on the sofa, our legs touching, his arm brushing mine as he turned a page. It was the most scary, happy feeling I could ever remember.

'These women were so dedicated,' marvelled Nick. 'Up and down those stairs in all weathers, all without pay. Who were the fairwives?'

'I don't know. Charlotte Ravell mentions them, and I think I saw a reference somewhere else. Where did you find them?'

Nick peered at the spidery writing on the page. 'Lost it now. But it was 1860 or so. Adele Ravell.'

'She's later than Charlotte. Must have been a daughter or daughter-in-law. I so need to go to the Records Office to make a list. Maybe the fairwives were helpers from the village. Maybe that was how the family referred to them.'

'Could easily be. The Fairlight being there is the sort of thing you accept, growing up in Whitcliff, but these accounts really bring home what an important part the leading lights played in the community.'

'Guarding Whitcliff by land and by sea,' I said lightly. 'It's what the Ravells have always done. It goes with the territory.'

'Even so, it's a tie. Someone would always have to stay in the house. All very well in the days of large families, not so good as the size dwindled in modern times. I should think they embraced GPS with open arms when it grew widespread, didn't they? No need to be on call for the Fairlight night and day any more.'

I exchanged a glance with Granny. 'Not all of them,' I said ruefully, thinking of Phyllis Ravell, jealously hoarding her diminished role. 'The Fairlight has always been ready in case of need. Looking after it is easy, compared to what the fishermen of the village go through out at sea. And those boats were bringing back fish for Fairlights as well as for themselves, don't forget.'

Nick was silent a moment. 'Community. That's the thing, isn't it? One for all. I suppose that's why I'm on the lifeboat crew when I'm home. Because I can.'

My hand crept to his. It came to me, horribly painfully, that I would die several deaths now whenever there was a call-out. *Welcome to the world, Sorcha.*

8

The building work proceeded much more smoothly without Tristram's interference. Left to himself, Alastair hardly bothered us at all. He divided his time between sea-angling and covering all the auction rooms and country house sales in the area, proving surprisingly adept at pouncing on period furniture at knockdown prices to store in the barns. I was beginning to consider the possibility that I'd misjudged him. Maybe he was simply a perfectionist who needed the real world explained to him at steady intervals. He bought his Edwardian staircase, Nick's men started to demolish the existing main tower stair. Nick and I gradually got to know each other.

It was getting colder now, with rain clouds blowing up increasingly frequently. 'How on earth am I going to fill bedrooms this time next year?' I mused aloud, staring out through the barn door at a near-vertical downpour. '*Come to Fairlights in Autumn: season of storms.*' I knew I could make the guest-experience lovely inside, but wall-to-wall wetness outside was quite a tricky sell.

'At this rate,' said Nick, scrubbing his hand through his hair as he surveyed the jigsaw of staircase sections piled up around the floor, 'you can bill it as a restoration workshop opportunity.'

I winced and turned back to him. 'Oh dear, is it that bad? I was hoping it was just me not understanding what slotted where.'

'All the pieces seem to be numbered in Alastair-speak. I knew I should have gone over there myself when he was arranging transportation. I'm an idiot.'

But looking at him, surrounded by old wood, all cream Aran and blue denim and tousled dark hair, a rather wonderful idea had come to me. 'No, you're not,' I said. 'You're a genius. Restoration weeks. That's exactly what we'll do. How are you at teaching?'

He shook his head sadly. 'Won't wash, Sorcha. I'm fairly sure there are regulations about having operational stairs *before* visitors arrive, not once they've finished making them.'

I grinned. 'Not the stairs, all this other furniture Alastair's been buying. Any guests who are interested could spend two or three days of their stay learning how to restore period furniture. They'd pay extra for the tuition. And if that took off, I could arrange a whole series of workshops on other crafts. Painting weeks, for example. People love them. Who's the artist who does those lovely watercolours in the Whitcliff Gallery? Then there are photography courses. Or . . . '

He cupped my cheek. 'Now who's the genius?'

★   ★   ★

Unfortunately Tristram returned three weeks later, his holiday apparently already a distant memory. My first reaction on hearing his voice was pure aggravation that he was back and would be getting in our way again. My second, following hard on the heels of the first, was violent nausea.

Out of sight, out of mind. Truest phrase in the universe. Not seeing Tristram on a daily basis, I'd managed very successfully to put what we had learnt from Laurel into a locked-away part of my head. As soon as he appeared in the doorway of my office, the lock burst open and shock and revulsion kicked in.

It was appalling. This was my eldest cousin, the leader since our earliest days, charming, good-looking, dynamic. And he had left me unconscious and bleeding on the pele stair. I had to physically grip the seat of my chair to stop myself hurtling down the passage and throwing up in the old scullery. As it was, there was such horror in me as I looked at his Armani suit, light tan and confident expression that the only sound to emerge

156

from my throat was a kind of death rattle.

'I want to know exactly where we're up to,' he said. 'Get everyone in the ballroom in five minutes.'

That one word *ballroom* broke through my paralysis. 'Restaurant,' I snapped. 'It's going to be the restaurant. Call the rooms by their proper names. I have the schedule right here, Tristram, there's no need for a progress meeting. You can't just disrupt routine by pulling craftsmen out of their jobs whenever you feel like it. That's a sure way to delay things.'

'Watch me,' said Tristram, smoothing his already impeccable blond hair. 'It's no skin off their noses. They're still getting paid. I'm simply reminding them who by.'

Ruthless, whispered a word in my head. *Selfish*, whispered another.

He crowed with justification when the lifeboat klaxon blasted from the harbour the very next moment, causing half the team to drop everything and set off at a run for the shoreline. 'There you are, you see?' he said. 'Unreliable. I knew it. Where's your *routine* now?'

I ignored him, racing outside after the men. 'Stay safe,' I called to Nick.

He twisted his head for a fleeting second, blowing me a kiss as he ran. My heart lifted in acknowledgement. I turned back to the house, to see Tristram stepping off the veranda, a look of black fury on his face.

'So, Alastair was right. I could hardly believe it when he mentioned it. Has the desperation caught up with you already, Sorcha? I did warn you.'

'Not in the least.' I tried to walk past him but he moved between me and the house. An old Tristram trick. I hadn't seen him do it for years.

'Body clock,' he sneered. 'Always the same with career women. You want it all and you're not getting any younger.'

His thin veneer of charm had gone. Had he been like this all along?

'It's funny how no one ever complains about men wanting it all,' I said pointedly. 'Leave me alone, Tris. My personal life is nothing to do with you. Nick and I are professionals. *If* we get together, it will make no difference to our working relationship, it will make no difference to how I run Fairlights. You'll still get your investment back.'

He took a step towards me. 'Not once you shack up with your bit of rough, I won't,' he snarled. 'You'll be too lovey-dovey to concentrate. It's slack enough as it is around here. I'm bringing in my own people, starting tomorrow. Maybe that will get things moving.'

White-hot rage engulfed me, both at the insults and the threat. 'No you bloody aren't. Fairlights is *my* project, *my* hotel, and things *are* moving. You would never even have thought of the idea if I hadn't suggested it. Don't mess with my business, Tris. I know precisely how to build up the hotel to give *years* of profit — not your flash-in-the-pan few months' worth before selling up. You are not going to bully me into tamely handing over control to you. I went through every word of that contract and I know exactly what you can and can't do.'

'You're a fool, Sorcha. You depend on me to even exist and it's time you realised it. No bank would have lent you the money. The family think you're mad to be converting Fairlights. They're expecting you to fail, do you realise that? Then they'll rally round with tissues and elastoplast and comfort blankets and say that at least you gave it your best shot. I could buy you out right now and bulldoze the place, like we should have done to begin with. It would be for your own good, saving you months of worry and stress. No one would blame me at all.'

Adrenalin blasted through my veins. It was as if all my ancestors had shot out of their graves at that word 'bulldoze' and were massed about me, buoying me up, belting out support. 'Over my dead body. You have no idea of the stink I could create if you made the slightest, tiniest move towards any such thing. I'm no longer fifteen years old, Tristram. Tell me, how long was it before you realised you were safe?'

I think we both felt the shock as the words left my lips. Dear God, what had got into me? I hadn't meant to mention anything until I was sure of my facts. By the look on his face, Tris had never expected me to mention it at all.

'I don't know what you mean,' he said, but there was a touch of calculation at the back of his eyes and he took another step towards me.

Bluff it out. 'No wonder you're so successful,' I said coolly. 'You must think the angels have been on your side for your whole life. Do you actually bank on your luck, Tris? You should. It's pretty impressive. I mean, of all the times for me to hit my head and lose my memory, it had to be then! It's astonishing.'

He took another step. I realised with reined-in hysteria that I was being manoeuvred towards the edge of the cliff. And still part of me was saying *This is Tris. This is your cousin. This cannot be happening.*

'You're raving, Sorcha. If I were you, I'd think very carefully before making allegations like that in public. They could so easily be misconstrued. Do you really want me to instruct my solicitor to pull my investment in the project? I've done it before.'

'Heaven help the poor saps who trust you. I'm warning you, Tristram, if you try to take Fairlights away from me and Granny, the whole family is going to know what happened that day.'

He threw back his head and laughed. Golden-haired, charming, insultingly confident. 'They won't believe you. You had severe concussion. It was fifteen years ago. Come on, Sorcha. Would you believe it?'

Weirdly, that anomaly cut through my fury and brought me up short. Why would the family not believe he had dared me to run up and down the pele stair? It was a very Tristram thing to have done. Why would they not believe he had panicked and run away when I fell? That was considerably more shameful, but just as likely. So what else had he done back then that he thought people might not believe?

'I had blood on my fingertips,' I said slowly, remembering Granny's description.

'The walls of the pele stair are stone. The steps are stone. You scraped your hands when you fell.'

Alarm bells rang in my head. That was too glib. Too practised. And also, not likely. My mind's eye imagined me stepping into the staircase, coming over terrified and trying to leave. By the door.

'The door,' I said on a thread of a breath. Now his eyes were shuttered. 'It was sticking.'

He'd locked it. He'd locked me in. I knew it as surely as if I'd seen his hand reach forward and turn the key. Bile rose in my throat, choking me. 'You didn't call an ambulance. You're right,

Tris, that takes some believing. If I had died, you would have been a murderer. And for what? Pride? Control? Some sort of petty revenge?'

I felt cold inside. Cold and steely and sick. 'Erin said you've had something on your mind since this project started, but it wasn't a woman at all, was it? It was your shoddy, mean, shameful secret. That's why you keep coming up here. It's not just to interfere. You're probing a sore tooth. It was fine when I was working miles away, making flying visits to check up on Granny. But living at Fairlights full time, seeing Nick Marten every day . . . You were afraid I'd remember. Terrified that if I got back together with him, it would trigger total recall. Did you unpack my bag for me too, by the way, that day?'

He took another step. Behind me, the sea sounded very close. How stupid was I? Picking a fight the one time when no one was out here, when no one was watching.

Another step. I must be so near the

edge now. I needed a plan. If I ran straight at him, I'd take him by surprise. I could dodge around him and get back to the house. I tensed my calf muscles, rose imperceptibly to the balls of my feat.

And then, incongruously, my mobile rang.

'False alarm, sweetheart. We're on our way back. Tell your cousin he's not bankrolling the lifeboat today.'

'Thanks,' I said, my eyes on Tristram. 'He'll be happy to hear that. I'm talking to him right now. I'm so glad no one was hurt. See you in a bit. I'll put the kettle on.'

I put the phone away and looked at Tristram.

Nothing. Silence.

'I'll tell you what, Tris,' I said. 'You stay well away from Fairlights from now on and I'll repay your financial input as soon as I possibly can. If you want to send Erin and the kids up here to visit Granny, that's fine, but I really don't want to see you, yourself, ever again.

Not ever, Tris.' And I walked past him back to Fairlights and my office.

★ ★ ★

At supper Tristram announced he'd be going back in the morning. He didn't meet my eyes, and I made no comment.

That night, though, I couldn't sleep. I lay awake replaying horror after horror in my head. He'd locked me inside the place of my nightmares. He hadn't called an ambulance. *If I'd died, he would have been a murderer.*

What was I to do? Heaven knows, there had been rotten apples in the Ravell clan before, but this was here, this was now, this was my cousin, the father of Erin's children. Yes, he was older than he'd been back then, more mature perhaps, but could I really just let it lie? How would I live with myself if his temper got the better of him again? My gaze rested on my door and I felt physically ill. For the first time ever at Fairlights I had bolted myself into my bedroom.

I lay and sweated and doubted, and the scenes went around in my head. I was on the pele stair, I was on the cliff top, I was falling, falling ... And through it all I could hear the wind steadily rising.

The next day required a lot of solid work with the makeup bag before I trusted myself to be seen at the breakfast table. Even so, Granny looked at me sharply, as if she was within an inch of ordering me back to bed.

Poached eggs on thickly buttered toast helped, as did tea. I took a second mug through to my office to snatch a quick word with Nick before work started for the day. Unfortunately, Tristram was in the hotel wing, pacing up and down the lobby, phoning for a cab to take him to the station.

'He'll be lucky,' murmured Nick. 'Does he not listen to the local news?'

He was right. The booking office repeated that trees had come down overnight on the main line and all trains were cancelled until at least this evening. The builders turning up for work confirmed that there were problems with the roads out of the village too.

'Great. Stuck in the middle of nowhere,' said Tristram with a glower. He looked broodingly at Alastair, preparing for a morning of sea fishing. 'I'll come with you,' he said abruptly. 'Nothing else to do here.'

Nick cast a troubled look across the veranda, at the lowering sky and white-crested waves. 'Donal?' he said into his phone. 'You aren't really going out?'

'If we're paying, he will be,' said Tristram.

Alastair looked up from his kit in amazement that the trip might be cancelled. 'It's a strong westerly! The fishing will be awesome.'

Apparently Nick's brother-in-law said much the same. 'Lunatic,' muttered Nick, sliding his mobile into his shirt pocket. 'He says it's rough, but safe enough. At least he's got the sense to cut and run for harbour if it really blows up.'

The sky grew darker during the morning, heavy clouds, charcoal-grey with menace, bringing fierce, squally rain. Everyone cast frequent glances towards the wind-whipped sea and conferred with each other in low voices. Soon after lunch, the power went off.

'The whole town is out,' reported Nick, coming into my office. 'They're saying it could be twenty-four hours until they get the repairs sorted. We can't do any more here today, Sorcha. I'm sending the guys home. I'd best go check on Ma. See if she needs me to pick up Jamie. Have you got enough coal and wood in?'

'Yes,' I said, following him out onto the veranda. The wind whipped my hair into my eyes. 'And even if we hadn't, I'm a big, strong girl. See you later if you can make it. I really have to talk to you about Tristram. I need your advice.'

'I'll do my best.' He dropped a kiss on my lips and left.

Granny had already got the paraffin

light going in the kitchen. As she put the kettle on the Aga, we heard the lifeboat klaxon. Both of us stiffened.

'Nick won't be back for a while yet then,' I said, trying not to let my voice shake. I pulled the Fairlight diaries across to give me something to concentrate on. Granny began chopping vegetables for soup for much the same reason.

Rain spattered against the window. I transcribed another of Hannah Ravell's accounts with the sound of the gale as a background. *The wind is very bad tonight*, Hannah had written, *but it must be tenfold worse for Edward and Ross. Mary and I take comfort from our duty.*

How had all those women lived like this? How had they kept going when their men faced danger every day on the water? I was thinking almost entirely of Nick. It wasn't until Granny handed me a bowl of soup to taste that I realised it was now late afternoon and Alastair and Tristram weren't yet back either. I didn't dare say anything to Granny — not with

Grandad's loss still fresh in her mind, even fifty years on.

My phone ringing suddenly into the silence was shocking. My pen skittered across the page and Granny's ladle fell with a splash into the soup pan.

'Sorcha, we've got a problem.'

'Nick?' I could hardly hear him for the wind noise on his mobile. 'Where are you? Are you okay?' I hadn't realised the human heart could beat so hard or fast.

His words filled me with dread. 'I'm with Donal on the *Kathryn May*. He's broken his arm and the boat's damaged, so I transferred across from the lifeboat. It's not at all clever out here. The lifeboat's gone off to another emergency.'

'But are you okay?'

'I'm fine. We've fixed Donal up as best we can. Alastair and your cousin are here to help with handling the boat. Listen, sweetheart, the GPS is kaput, the sea is all over the place, the rain is sheeting down and with the power

171

outage in Whitcliff, I can't see a bloody thing. I need you to light the Fairlight.'

I was already on my feet. 'Of course. I'll ring you when it's going. Stay safe, Nick. Please stay safe.'

I choked out an explanation to Granny, then grabbed my big coat from the porch and dashed through the passage into the pele tower. I'd hit the lift button and was zipping myself up before I realised that of course the lift wouldn't run without electricity. Cursing my stupidity at wasting even a couple of seconds, I spun towards the main staircase. And skidded to an appalled halt, my hand going to my mouth.

Because there was no main staircase. There was no staircase for two floors. The old one had been ripped out and the new one was still in erratically numbered sections, laid out on the floor of the barn.

9

I don't think I have ever panicked quite so hard in my life. I pelted back, fumbling for my ring of keys, passing Granny at the passage to the kitchen. 'I have to use the pele stair,' I gasped. 'Oh Granny, I don't know if I can.' But the image of Nick, battling a Force Nine sea in a damaged boat, forced my fingers to jam the key in the pele stair door and pull it open.

Terror swept through me. The open stone spiral was treacherous and dangerous and the scene of all my nightmares. And of course it was dark again. The fading light outside couldn't penetrate through the tower's narrow, defensive windows. I was very aware that the last time I'd been on these stairs I had fallen and lost my memory.

'Here,' said Granny, passing me a lit hurricane lantern.

Nick's voice came back to me. '*It's no worse than the cliff steps, Sorcha. I've seen you run up and down those hundreds of times.*' I made myself breathe. In. Out. I grasped the rope rail with my right hand and held the lantern in my left to illuminate the steps. The yellow light swung wildly, reinforcing my nightmare. My legs buckled.

You are not alone, sister, said a musical voice in my ear. *I've done this all my life. Put your feet where I put mine. Trust me.*

I nearly dropped the lantern! That was Grace! Grace Ravell. It really was. I felt her name run through my bones, knew it in the knowledge her voice somehow conveyed. The woman who had kept an open brazier going for the entirety of two storm-wracked days several centuries ago was guiding me up the pele stair! But how could she?

Somehow I got my foot onto the first stone step. The next step jutted above it. *Trust me,* urged Grace in my head. *Give your feet to mine. Be me.*

Madness. I was hallucinating in my terror.

Trust me, said Grace again. So I did. I went clear through the terror and out the other side. I gave myself completely to my ancestress's guiding shade. There *was* no other choice, not if I wanted to save Nick. I let her take me and within seconds, I no longer knew whether I was holding Granny's hurricane lantern or Grace's blazing torch. I was climbing, getting closer to the Fairlight, *not falling, not falling, not falling* . . .

And in the swirling light and dense shadows as I pushed myself higher, I realised that *this, now*, was what I had experienced at Grace's statue on my first night home. I'd known it had been a precognition, not a memory. It followed that this, now, had also been a precog when I was tiny. I had come into the pele stair as an adventurous five-year-old and been enveloped in the first and most intense foreknowledge I have ever experienced. No wonder I'd screamed blue murder. No wonder the black-yellow-swirling-choking vision had fed my nightmares for years. I hadn't been old enough or experienced enough to recognise it for what it was.

I climbed on, gripping the rope rail, keeping my eyes on the next ledge up, not thinking about the sheer drop down the centre of the spiral or how far there was to fall. Had I experienced this climb again as a fifteen-year-old after Tristram had locked the bottom door? Was that why I'd fallen and knocked myself out? I would never know — but it no longer mattered. Nick and I would go on and make new memories. He'd said so. I just had to get him home safe.

Home. Safe. I faltered as the enormity of the burden hit me. *Nearly there, sister*, hummed Grace in my head. The warmth of her confidence carried me up the last few dizzying turns to the roof.

In Grace's day, of course, there had been no inner gates on the pele stair. She withdrew silently from me at the top, leaving me to deal with this stage

176

alone. I put the lantern down and wrestled with the bolt on the door. It was stiff and difficult to budge. 'Oh, come on,' I shouted furiously at it. I hadn't climbed all this way to be thwarted by a lump of metal. There was a truly horrible moment when I had to let go of the rope rail and haul the inner grille open with both hands, but I did it. I got the outer door unlocked, staggered dangerously backwards with my arms wheeling for a heart-stopping moment, and then threw myself forward in a sweating scramble straight into the howling, rain-drenched gale on the roof. Never have I been more pleased to be out in a storm. I fetched up hard against the tower crenellations and paused for just a second to steady my legs and catch my breath before putting my head down and pulling myself around them one by one until I reached the cupola.

The wooden walls creaked. One of the shutters was banging. But I was back on home ground. I could do this.

My thigh muscles were on fire and my breath was tearing in my chest. I didn't care. Compared to that nightmare climb, this was easy. I grasped the rail above the three steps leading to the cupola, set my hand to the door and I was inside.

I wanted to weep with relief, but there was no time for even a moment's weakness. With hands that really didn't seem to belong to me, I lit the Fairlight and set it on the platform, thanking all the gods that about a thousand years ago I'd sat up here with Nick readying the lamp and priming the spares.

Then, finally, I slumped to the floor, reaction hitting me. I fumbled my phone out. 'It's lit,' I said to Nick.

'Bless you,' he said. There was a faint shout behind him. 'I see it. Christ, we're way off course. Keep it going.'

I sat on the floor of the cupola with my back to a bench, shaking violently. On the far side of the roof, the hurricane lamp that I'd left on the top step of the pele stair glowed, but one thing I knew. Nothing was shifting me from this spot until Nick — and anyone else caught in the storm — was safely in harbour. I recalled a line from one of the journals: '*You can read about it, you can be told it by someone who was there, but until you are on the roof of the pele, just you and the Fairlight defying the elements, you don't feel it within yourself. You don't know.*' I had never read a truer paragraph.

Suddenly there was the shriek of wood as a particularly vicious gust tore the door from its hinges. My heart hammered as the door flew over the crenellations, splintering as it went, shards of glass making a glittering shower intermixed with the wind and the rain. Around me, the other walls creaked and fractured, one weakness creating others.

I scrambled upright. The box seats were safe, bolted to the floor. I threw myself on the seat holding the spare lanterns, trying to remember which one it was where the oil, wicks and matches were stored. Another gust took two walls out, smashing the wood against the parapet. My heart ached for Charlotte Ravell as Robin's creation was flung piecemeal to the skies.

My phone rang again. 'It's all right, the lamp is still going,' I shouted. 'If you lost it, it was because the cupola is breaking up! It's mostly gone now, so the light should be clearer.'

But it wasn't Nick, it was Tristram. 'Listen,' he said, 'that day — '

No! Tris truly beggared belief. In the midst of a screaming storm, where people's *lives* were at stake, he wanted to justify his actions.

'Jeez, Tris, I'm a bit busy here,' I shouted.

'I *know*,' he yelled back. 'It's pretty bloody frantic out here too.'

'Well, get off the phone and help Nick then!'

'In a minute. I have to tell you first. In case we don't make it.'

'Tris!'

He ignored me. 'That day . . . '

Dear God. 'Yes? That day?'

'I locked you in the pele tower to

180

teach you a lesson. I was livid. No one ever crossed me the way you did. I listened to you screaming and clawing at the door, and I didn't care. Then you yelled that you would hate me for ever and I heard you start to climb the stair. You were still shouting, still sobbing, but I could hear you getting fainter. So I unlocked the door, left it a tiny bit open, so I could pretend it was all your imagination that it had been stuck, and I left. I left, Sorcha. *I bloody left, do you hear?* I put your bag in your room to irritate you, then I got in the car and drove to the agricultural show to join the family. I didn't know you'd fallen, I didn't know you'd hit your head. When I got back and realised, I had to bolt for the loo to throw up. Everyone was racing around worried about you. No one even thought I might have been the last person to see you. I was so ill, thinking I was going to be crucified when you came round. I couldn't believe my luck when you woke up and you'd lost your memory.'

His voice stopped. In the background I could hear the wind, hear the crashing sea. I could hear Nick steadily swearing. And then the line went dead.

Typical, I thought, but even that was at a distance, as if my mind was dredging up a suitable response. Tristram chooses the one time when his great revelation is of less interest to me than dodging lethal flying planks on top of a hundred-foot-high tower, whilst concentrating on a pocket handkerchief of ocean several miles out to sea. I put the phone in my pocket and him out of my mind. *Come on, Nick*, I willed, straining my eyes at the huge, chaotic, wildly crashing waves. *Steer for the light. I'm not going to lose you just when we've found each other.*

To my horror, there was a rattle as the Fairlight rocked dangerously on its pedestal. Oh *stupid* Sorcha! It was no longer sheltered from the wind! I leapt and grabbed it. Hell, that had been close. It had to be in this one place or Nick wouldn't be able to line it up above the Outer Light in the harbour. I chanted the rhyme under my breath, aiming the words directly at Nick. '*Outer to port, Fairlight ahead, bring them together, home you are led.*' The wind buffeted me. I snarled at it to back off. I would hold this lamp here all night if I had to.

So much for grand vows. After twenty minutes my arms were in agony. Why hadn't Robin thought to include a bloody chair in his design? Worse, I was suffering from hallucinations again. Crazy as it seemed, I had the sense of other women on the roof with me. They were at my back. They surrounded me. I gritted my teeth and darted a look sideways to stare them down.

What the . . . The wind nearly knocked me off balance at what I saw. I gripped the Fairlight and looked again. It was true! I *wasn't* imagining it! A beautiful girl stood there, her blue hood fallen back and her blonde hair streaming behind her in the wind. She glanced at me with an impish expression as if she knew exactly what I was thinking, before laying her arm along the top of mine, giving me strength to keep the lamp steady. My mind whirled in disbelief, because I knew this blue-cloaked girl from the drawing of the cupola. She was Charlotte Ravell, 1812, wife of Robin. I felt warmth along my other arm and whipped my head to the left. Another woman stood there, this one shorter and stouter, well wrapped in a thick plaid shawl. She turned and smiled. *Hannah*, she said in my head, before returning her steady gaze to the sea. Ranged behind them on both sides, other women in all manner of cloaks, coats and scarves nodded at me.

The fairwives! Oh, my heavens, the fairwives! A giddy, ridiculous gladness seized me. Now I understood all those entries in the Fairlight accounts. And now I understood why none of them ever stated who exactly the fairwives were.

Surrounding me were all the women who had ever looked after the Fairlight. All of them. Drawn forward somehow through the centuries to the pele tower whenever one of their number was in need.

'Thank you,' I said aloud, hearing the sob in my voice. I looked around through the tears in my eyes and felt a massive surge of sisterhood. All these women, united in getting their men home safely. United again now, for me and mine.

All but one. On the edge of the group stood an angular shadow, stiff and unyielding. I recognised her stance from old family photographs. Phyllis, the woman who had made Granny's life a torment. Scornful, overbearing, never admitting she needed help. Unwilling to share her miser's hoard of knowledge.

There was a murmur from the fair-wives, a sharpening of attention. I sucked in my breath as I searched ahead. Yes! I could see something! Out at sea there was a flickering light, now there, now gone.

'Nick?' I said aloud. 'Nick?'

And then my blood ran cold, because the Fairlight was dimming. 'No,' I screamed. 'I'm running out of oil!' If he lost the leading lights, Nick would smash the boat on the offshore rocks. He was depending on me to keep it going. I knew what I needed to do, but how? I had spare lamps, I had supplies, I had the fairwives' strength. What I didn't have were a second pair of real live hands to light the fresh lamp.

Or did I? Over by the stair, the women were moving aside. The lone, angular shadow stiffened with incredulity. Something — someone — was crawling across the roof, muttering under her breath the whole time.

'I saw the cupola walls crashing past the window onto the ground,' said Granny, her eyes tight shut. 'And then when I looked, I saw the light at the top of the stair. I couldn't bear it downstairs on my own, Sorcha, not again. I thought if you were brave enough to beat your horrors, then I could be too.' She shook her head wonderingly. 'So strange. All the way up, I knew I was doing it right. Last time, I knew it was wrong. Show me where you need me. I heard you call out.'

I cried aloud with relief. 'Oh, you marvellous woman. Oh, Granny, you marvellous, marvellous woman. Pull yourself upright and stand next to me. The lamp is going out. Just hold it steady while I light the new one. The wind will fight you for it, so you need to hang on.'

'I've been hanging on all my life,' she said, still not opening her eyes. 'If I don't look, I can manage. Who's here with us, Sorcha? I can feel something warm.'

'It's the fairwives,' I said with a half-sob, half-laugh, for her prosaic tone. 'It really is. It's Hannah and Charlotte and Adele and everyone. All the women who came before us. It was them got you back last time.'

She nodded. 'Thankee kindly,' she said, still not looking.

I got out a spare lamp and lit it with clumsy, frozen hands. The wick took, burned steadily. 'I'm going to swap the lamps over,' I told Granny. 'Get ready.' I put the new one in front of the old just as the light from the first one died.

'I've done it,' I said. 'You can take the

old one down and put it in the seat to your left. It lifts.' I caught my breath. 'Oh, Granny, I think I see them. They're not that far outside the harbour now.' Briefly there, briefly gone, but there was no mistaking it. A storm-tossed boat, ridiculously small against the open sea. I wondered if my heart rate would ever return to normal.

Granny let go, felt her way to the bench seat, and from there slid to the ground. 'Somebody else is going to have to get me down,' she said.

You and me both, Granny.

'The boat is getting closer,' I called, after what seemed an eternity. 'It's nearly at the harbour entrance. Oh, come on, Nick. Come on.' There were tears smeared over my cheeks, hot for the tiniest instant before being diluted by the rain and blasted to ice by the wind.

It wasn't just me, the fairwives were crooning encouragement too. Out of the corner of my eye I saw Phyllis, a black shadow to one side, look silently at Granny, then come slowly forward to join them.

My phone rang one last time. 'I thought you'd like to know Alastair says he sees the point of the Fairlight now,' said Nick. 'I love you, Sorcha. I'm coming in.'

The boat was moving steadily in the calmer waters of the harbour. I closed my eyes in thankfulness, sobbing with reaction. When I opened them and looked again, the *Kathryn May* had disappeared under the shadow of the cliff. We were there. We'd done it.

The fairwives faded away like a gentle, warm caress. I would write this, I vowed. I would write this in the accounts. My daughters, my sons' wives, they would need to understand. Because the fairwives were still there, layered in the past. I could feel them in my soul. Some day I would be one of them.

'They've made it, Granny,' I said. 'He'll be here soon.'

Still I stayed holding the Fairlight, until figures appeared at the door of the pele stair. Alastair got Granny to her feet, ready to help her down the steps, but I had eyes for only one person.

He was tall, dark and impossibly good-looking, despite the battering he'd got from the storm. He was also swaying with tiredness, wet, cold, and reeking of salt and diesel. I had a suspicion I wasn't in any much better condition myself.

'Dear God, I love you, Nick Marten,' I said. 'You had better not be planning on going back this evening. I want you next to me all night long. Where we both belong.'

His eyes never left mine. He took out his phone. 'Hi Ma, it's Nick. We're all safe, but I won't be home tonight. I'm staying with Sorcha.' He reached out a hand to me. 'Possibly for ever.'

THE END

MISTRESS OF MELLIN COVE

Rena George

When Dewi Luscombe is rescued from a shipwreck by the young Master of Mellin Hall, Kit St Neot, she finds she has lost her memory and doesn't know who she is. Touched by the girl's vulnerability and confusion, Kit decides to help her. But Dewi is haunted by the thought that someone close to her died in the shipwreck, and she sets off with Kit to ride across Cornwall to discover her true identity. Will Dewi ever regain her memory? And will Kit return her growing feelings for him?

SWEET VENGEANCE

Roberta Grieve

Aspiring actress Kelley Robinson mistakes infatuation for love when she falls for charismatic media celebrity Carl Roche. Despite the warnings of her friends, she believes his promises and moves in with him. But when she discovers how he has deceived her, she is determined to get her revenge. Paul, a seemingly sympathetic journalist, offers to help put her plan into action. But is he only looking for a good story for his newspaper? Who can Kelley really trust?

ONWARD AND UPWARD

Chrissie Loveday

It is 1953, and the Cobridge family is ever-growing. Paula and William have settled in their flat, and Nellie and James's daughter Bella is becoming a rebellious youngster. As her teacher, Paula believes she is suffering from dyslexia. She also thinks the child is somewhat neglected by her overly busy parents. William is engaged in his coronation ware at the ceramics factory and all seems to be moving onward — until disaster suddenly hits the family. How will Nellie survive alone?